excerpt from

SMEDLEY's
Secret Guide to World Literature

By Jonathan Levy Wainwright, age 15.6

Askold Melnyczuk

Also by Askold Melnyczuk

The House of Widows

Blind Angel

Ambassador of the Dead

What Is Told

As Editor:

Conscience, Consequence: On Father Daniel Berrigan

On Bergstein

From Three Worlds: New Writing from Ukraine (co-editor)

Take Three Poetry Series (Graywolf)

As Translator:

Girls
by Oksana Zabuzhko

Eight Notes from a Blue Angel
by Marjana Savka

excerpt from
SMEDLEY's
Secret Guide to World Literature
By Jonathan Levy Wainwright, age 15.6

PFP, INC
publisher@pfppublishing.com
PO Box 829
Byfield, MA 01922

April 2016
Printed in the United States of America

© 2016 -Askold Melnyczuk

First PFP edition © 2016

ISBN-10:0-9970248-1-X
ISBN-13:978-0-9970248-1-4
(also available in eBook format)

Front cover image:
Pietre Valbuena - www.pietrevalbuena.com

Excerpts from *Smedley's Secret Guide* have appeared in *The Drum,* Baum's Bazaar, and *Ropes* as well as in a chapbook from Anomalous Press and in *The Los Angeles Review of Books*

My thanks to:
Henriette Lazaridis, Jamie Clarke, Molly McLaughlin and Erica Mena.

To the rebel soul in everyone

& of course

For Alex

CONTENTS

Beyond the Calculus of Dreams

Beyond the Calculus of Dreams

I dislike holidays. Everyone knows Coke colorized Santa. And I've read that Anna Jarvis, who invented Mother's Day in tribute to her mom, a peace activist and nurse to both sides in the Civil War, disowned it when Hallmark started selling cards. Even Halloween creeps me out.

I make an exception for Memorial Day. Not that I ever go to a parade or cheer the canons roaring in the park or sing the rousing hymns. Parades are not my thing either. But who can say he never hears a summons from the dead? That day, wherever I am, I always find a way to slip off by myself.

Alone, I think back to that weekend in late May when my world shifted in a way I'd never dreamed my life might go. If I happen to be home, I dig up the document I wrote when I was fifteen. Sometimes I even tinker with it.

I'd run into a little trouble at school and had taken refuge with my godfather in Manhattan. I wonder what my life would be had I stayed home. I'd never have met Beyah, or learned my godfather's secret, or seen, too late, as it turned out, just who my mother had really been. I wouldn't be writing this. But the future tense didn't exist for me then, and I could hardly be said to have much of a past. *Now* was all that mattered, since *now* was all that was.

excerpts from
SMEDLEY's
Secret Guide to World Literature

By Jonathan Levy Wainwright, age 15.6

I'm lucky to be alive. Standing in the principal's office in Cambridge last week, listening to the charges against me, I could feel Dad's blood pressure blow through the roof. This was no time to be tipping the family boat—mainly because it had already capsized. The ever-clueless Dr. Post droned on about my "crimes against humanity." Truth is, I felt fine. The stuff these old guys get away with...They were just trying to scare me. Part my cheeks before the stun-gun dildo of authority until it drilled into my brain and bending over became an addiction. Say *Thank you, sir.* Maybe: *Wedge the boot in deeper, sir—yum!* But what was their worst? As it was late May already, the Principalities and Powers decided I should take the rest of the year, plus summer, to reflect on my sins.

"Since you love the web so much," Dad said when we got home—his voice softly savage—"Why don't you learn how to use it correctly?" Looking at him, I wondered: was this my future? The shaved head and green eyes of a hairless cat-Dr. Spock hybrid. Weird, even for a published, neo-formalist poet. Then, like the good big professor he is, he gave me an assignment. I am condemned to write an essay on the importance of literature in the age of Twitter. Five thousand words, minimum. His last sabbatical we lived in Rome, where he wanted me to talk to him in Latin. *Ita,* baby, *ita.*

After my suspension, because things at home are so crazy these days, I asked Dad if I could go stay with my god-father, Henry, in New York for a while. He had a stroke a few months ago which left him partly paralyzed. As the GF has no family of his own (how did he work that, I wonder?), I thought he might be lonely. He was always fun, and I'm hoping the stroke hasn't changed that. But I wasn't sure what the 'rents would say. Just last week Mom called him a sell-out. A lot of people are sell-outs in Mom's eyes. Very few mortals meet her standards. She gives the "thumbs up" to only a handful.

To my surprise, Mom said it would do me good to help take care of someone else for a change. For the first time in ages, Dad agreed.

But I also have the Virgins to think of. It's ten days to Memorial Day. The Vocal Virgins—Klyt, Astro, and my girl-friend, Rene—have been rehearsing like crazy for the Battle of the Bands. As I'm manager *and* lead songwriter, though still working on my first tune, I see mucho skyping in my future.

* * *

Holed up in my room, Syphilitic Vagina on my pod, I immediately get down to making up a Table of Contents for my *Secret Guide*. Because Dad's a poet who teaches and grades hard, this will take planning. Key to prose: the forespice of surprise.

Mom was sure surprised when Dad made his announcement a few months back. I guess she thought they'd stay married forever—though she said she knew something was wrong when he became obsessed with reruns of *The Dukes of Hazzard*. Reruns mess with your mind. They make you think you are the age you were when you saw the dumb show in the first place. This is only a theory. But I bet I could get a PhD for it. Rene claims she expected this all along.

* * *

Not all men are equally capable of keeping it in their pants, I think, as I stretch out in bed while the sun sinks behind the pines outside my window.

I roll the sleeping bag up and push it under the pillow. Mom quit the housework racket some years ago. First it was laundry; then, cooking. Who could blame her? Washing underwear and heating chickens from the local deli will take it out of anyone. Needless to say, Dad wasn't about to pick up the slack. To streamline things, Asia and I were issued sleeping bags and given lessons in the proper use of the microwave. I have no objections. It's all training, far as I'm concerned. I know I'm lucky to have a place to sleep, in a safe part of town.

I was talking to Matiop outside of school a few weeks back. Matiop's from Sudan. He learned English by writing the alphabet in the sand. His parents were killed in the civil war there. He's only a freshman, even though he's eighteen. He told me how the war changed the way the rats behaved. It seems the homes of the rats kept being destroyed by bombs and people running over them. They must have realized they had to defend themselves, so they began to get aggressive. They organized into gangs. They roamed the streets in packs, attacking people in daylight. He said he watched a baby abandoned by its mother eaten alive by three rats the size of large cats.

Now that was tough.

And the stuff I've seen on the web I wish I could unsee: beheadings, incest, rapes. The things people will do, given the chance. Makes you wonder if we're all just waiting for the right moment to go nuts. I used to think that nothing terrible could happen to you if someone was there making a movie because the cameraman would stop it. Right?

Last week I watched a video of a kitten ripped apart by a raccoon in someone's back yard. What kind of a person films that without trying to stop it?

Klyt's father, actually. It was Klyt who showed us that. His old man had posted it to YouTube.

If ever I do forget my privileges, my friends quickly remind me. Rene, Astro, even Klyt, love pointing out that I have the edge on just about everyone. I am a privileged white boy. A potential master of the universe. But can I tell you something? Seriously, if this is how good luck feels, then, oh man, everybody else must sure be sucking the big one.

Unfortunately, the Table of Contents page for my project remains blank.

Downstairs, Mom and Dad scream at each other over a soundtrack of late Miles. "You really think I believe...." "And the smoking...." "Pig!" I sit up and take a deep, deep breath.

* * *

My name is Jonathan Levy Wainwright, but I go by Smedley. I'll explain later. I was born during the so-called "Clinton era"—though that seems to overemphasize his importance, because what did the dude accomplish, really? A financial bubble. A book deal that drove Dad ballistic. Yet even Mom thought he was hot. Rene's sure he's into sexting. Imagine getting a tongue sign from Bill, she said. Many of my classmates credit him with inspiring the new sexual revolution. It's a legacy all right. Sex is an occupational hazard of living.

The shouts downstairs grow louder. I get up and look out the window at the empty koi pond below. The lining sprang a leak last summer, draining the water. I woke up one morning to find the fish scattered across the crusty bottom like withered orange peels. All it took was a pinprick.

I look at the books on my shelf. You know how many writers there are in the world? And Dad thinks he's a big-shot? I was ready to blow off this dumb gig but then I thought hey, Dad creams over writers like they're his rectal version of The Clash or The Decembrists. He thinks of course I'll mess this up, so why not show him how it's done?

While we're on the subject, let me say outright: I'm a big believer in homosexuality. What I mean is, people are who they are and they should stay that way—even if sometimes surgery is required to get them there. But when your dad decides to come out of the closet at fifty-five, and you are fifteen years old, and your girlfriend just might be pregnant, no one is happy. This goes back to my philosophy that people should stay who they are. But they seem determined not to, and it's hard to adjust. Take me, for instance. I am famously undergoing many hormonal changes. I could almost grow a fucking moustache overnight, if I wanted. This will surely help me get laid in the future. Right now, though, I've got a big problem with Rene.

Gay's no biggie these days, especially for a poet, where it's practically a professional necessity, and in Cambridge, Massachusetts, where I live, it's more rule than exception. But it's a blow to learn a person is not who they appeared to be all your life. Seems people don't always know who they are even when they're old. And Dad was never interested in anything except poets, poetry, and apparently, desk clerks. In fact, my problem is, being gay is *so* cool these days, at least in this city, that if I say anything critical, it's like I'm calling Jesus a child molester.

Really, it's just that it's a shock. When I'm old, will I also care less how my kids feel? Maybe.

At last the shouting stops. A post-atomic silence settles over the house. Suddenly my own breathing sounds like the sea. I imagine Mom in the kitchen, furiously smoking a Lucky. And Dad? Ah, Dad! I wait for the slam of the door. Yep, there he is, getting on his bicycle, rolling into the twilight. Off to visit his clerk at the Charles, maybe. It's the night of the living dad, and has been for a while. Poor mom will sleep alone again tonight.

Not that she's so innocent either. I've heard the things they've said to each other. I can't figure her out any more than I get him, or they me. Welcome to my family.

It's funny how, except for Rene, the rest of us hate our parents. Yet if they were to die suddenly, we'd probably be *verklempt.*

"You don't know the half of it," says Rene.

"You were adopted when you were eight months old," I point out. "You don't remember your family of origin. You don't remember anything."

I don't rub it in, don't remind her that her parents *gave her away.* Wonder when that'll start happening here. Way things are going, people will soon be bidding for babies on e-bay.

"I remember everything," she replies, giving me a look that makes me want to shake the marrow from a bone. To be fair, the girl has a remarkable memory. She can practically recite all the presidents forward and backward while solving quadrilateral equations and strumming a guitar. I appreciate her qualities. I do. After all, she shimmers like a disco ball.

She also claims I don't hate my parents. Says I'm spoiled and don't know much about the world. She says it often. She, of course, knows everything.

Yet it's a fact that my mother is a little insane. If my father is crazy because he is a poet, my mother is because she is not. I know most teenage boys think this about their mothers. We did a poll and Klyt and Astro sided with me. Rene remains the grateful one, saved from a Chinese orphanage by the benevolent white man. Only consider: ever since returning from Mac-Lean's, my mother, who is drop-dead gorgeous, has begun shouting randomly. Seems random, anyway. A Tourette's-like bark-scream combo. It's not a sound to help you down your dinner. There she goes now. Time for the headphones.

There's more. One day Mom took Dad's collection of rare manuscripts—handwritten letters by Rilke, Wordsworth, and Baudelaire—and made origami swans out of them. Mom's skilled that way. She is an incredible origamist.

But numero uno on the short list of her symptoms appeared six months ago, when she began pulling out her own teeth. Two of them, anyway. She said she'd chewed more than she'd bitten off, and that she never wanted to draw blood again. By which I think she meant she knows she analyzes everything to death. Mom has teeth and claws for judging folk.

I say this realizing full well how little I know about the old ones. The world they're so busy destroying is the manor to which I was born. But I've been kept to one room, and even there my powers are few. I listen to the sounds of destruction, the snapping of bones and breaking of hearts, the clatter of wood and shattering glass, as our home collapses around us, but what of it? None of my business, I'm told—until I inherit their mess.

I return to the Table of Contents and stare, mind blank as the page.

* * *

Notes for song: "Our goal is freedom." "Lips that smell of stale milk."

* * *

The next evening, as I'm getting ready to leave for New York, Rene stops by. She always insists on coming in to say hello. She's wearing her purple Hillary Headband and a tight, purple-striped t-shirt. A crucifix her mother bought her in Assisi hangs around her neck.

Dad's prepping for his class in the living room with the television on. He's working on a sonnet sequence based on an imaginary reality TV show and is a tireless researcher. I'm sure *The Dukes of Hazzard* will find its way into it. When he sees who it is, he mumbles hello and turns back to the set. He's embarrassed. He knows Rene knows.

Mom's in the kitchen, smoking—she's the last woman in North Cambridge with a habit—while designing a flier for one of her insane political groups on the Mac. The Scourge of the West, Dad calls her. She's wearing her thick blue cardigan even though the night is warm. But mom, who's skinny as a praying mantis, is always cold.

"Where you going?" she asks, flicking ash.

"Just the studio," I say. The "studio" is the unfinished apartment above my parents' garage.

Mom always takes my breath away. Her contacts blue her green eyes deeper than heaven. Her bones speak thoroughbreds and champagne. Then she starts talking and the truth comes out. Her father ran a fur storage company. Her mother was born in the Bronx. Her parents didn't approve her marrying outside the tribe. She told me this one bad night. Maybe they were right. They bought me my first bicycle, a black Mercier Kilto. Then they died. Conventional Mom never was. When I was a kid, she'd wait for me outside school, chain-smoking. Walking home, she'd rehearse her grievances with Dad. Once, she asked me if I'd like to live on a houseboat. Sure, I said. The next day, she enrolled me in swimming lessons at the Y. Scored perfect on her LSATs but went to Guatemala instead of law school. Both of my parents think their lives are so fascinating, I'm barely on their radar. Even now.

"Good evening, Mrs. Wainwright," Rene beams.

Mom nods, "Hello, Rene."

"How are you feeling, Mrs. Wainwright?"

Rene engages everybody. She talks to bus drivers, hall monitors, cashiers. I've seen her whispering to dogs, cats, birds and squirrels; once I even caught her babbling to a yellow jacket. Rene knows Mom's been sick. Unfortunately, she doesn't understand how seriously fucked things are around here.

Stubbing out the cig, Mom looks up. Her tiny pupils zap us like tasers: "Well thank you for asking. Nobody around here seems to care. Love is a house of pain, my dear." She pauses, adding: "An epiphany of pain!" She focuses on me.

I stare at my boots. Rene smiles like she's selling zircon on QVC.

Mom adds: "This one's all right. But you watch your back anyway."

When I was two, Mom put me in a backpack and carried me up Mount Wachusett. There's a photograph of me on the fridge wearing a fur hat, oversized gloves, and a red-and-black scarf, balanced on a snow-covered boulder, suave as a penguin, and about to hurl a snowball at the photographer. The witness to a life no one else around here seems to recall.

"You haven't finished packing," Mom reminds me, turning back to the computer. She's keen on the details of travel, always on me, making sure I've got toothpaste, socks, underwear—like I was heading for Siberia or something. Then she says, this time to Rene: "Never trust a poet!"

Sound advice. The bang of the screen door echoes down the warm night.

The studio is where Rene, Astro, Klyt and I—i.e., The Vocal Virgins—rehearse. Here we also debate the big questions, like: what's better: anarchy, democracy, or dictatorship? Astro, who always has the best weed, which has nothing to do with his being of African-American ancestry and living in the projects on Harvard Street in Cambridge surrounded by professional drug dealers, favors dictatorship. Rene, whose parents adopted her from China when she was eight months old, feels the typical immigrants' gratitude to liberal democracy. Me, I say: brothers and sisters, kick out the jams. Take the very doors off their hinges.

Our drummer Klyt, alas, doesn't have much of a clue.

Now Rene and I sit in the dark, on opposite sides of the room, on the floor. I fiddle with the microphone Rene normally plays with like a whip. Our equipment lies scattered where we left it after our last rehearsal: a couple of Fenders, the Olds cornet I'm desperately practicing, to impress Rene. She gave me a book by the Dead Musician, Miles Davis—DM/MD, i.e.—who is also a favorite of mom's (coincidence? Or is it like a poet Dad's always quoting said: *No accidents!* ?). Anyway, who has time to read while penning a survey of world literature? But I can't think about this now. We are facing catastrophe.

Every so often Rene turns my way, running her tongue over her lips like she's trying to remember my name. Like she can't quite finger me in a line-up, even though I'm the only one here.

Except for the occasional car horn from Mass Ave a few blocks away, the only sounds come from the mice in the walls. Salt-waves tumble down the skylight. Shadows spill across the space between us which might otherwise feel intolerably empty and still. The silence speaks of future mysteries, the hot gasp of tears, and other lyrical crap.

Like all girls, Rene has powers I can't begin to fathom. For example, she can, with a touch, or even a look, but usually it involves a gentle collision of foreheads, pass images from her mind to mine. The other day we were alone in the studio and she was telling me about a twin sister her American parents were unable to adopt—they've told her everything, more than she needed to know, maybe. She said that when she closes her eyes she can see the girl as clearly as, with eyes open, she sees me. Her sister was okay, she said. She was more than safe: she was royalty. Royalty, I said, in communist China? Communist shmomunist, Rene smiled. But she wasn't in China. No? No, she was in India. India? She'd been adopted by an Indian maharajah. A maharajah! Yes, she lived in a palace. One of many.

Look for yourself, she said. Where? Here.

She leaned over and touched my wrist, her finger falling

where a small vein knocked against the thin skin like a miniature and misplaced heart. At once I saw, or think I saw, a girl
riding an elephant. Layered in jewels, rubies, emeralds and diamonds, she wore bright gold robes webbed in veils of purple
gauze. Even the elephant was decked out, its ears studded with
lapis, a gold ring at the lip of its trunk. Whoa, that's your sister,
I said. That's her, she nodded, smiling. "And one day, I'll find
her." And I was sure she would. Then Rene added: With help
from the whales. Whales? Yes, the whales of Baja, California.

See, Rene thinks the world's creatures are trying to speak.
They're reaching out to warn us of dangers ahead. Apparently
the whales of Baja swim right up to tourist boats. They let
themselves be petted; people ride them. The whales know all
that's happened not only in the oceans but on the land and in
the air for as long as they've been around—and that's pretty
damn long.

And if you think this is crazy, let me say that I do too, but
Rene is very persuasive. Would the sanest person on the planet
believe something so completely nuts if it weren't true? We
have plans to go to Baja one of these days. At the same time,
Rene has this thing about dogs—maybe it's because she's Chinese, who knows. It bothers her how people treat them like
children while eating chickens and ignoring all the other creatures. Calls it animal racism. Says dogs are imperialists. Imperialist dog! Isn't that supposed to be Imperialist Pig? I asked, and
she said if it is, it's wrong. Dogs always want to be "top dog."

See, when you get involved with a girl, the mysteries of the
world begin to ripen. I mean it, no joke. It's addictive.

17

"Aren't you going to say anything?" Rene finally breaks the silence.

"I'll miss you?" I say.

"You're such a dick," she snaps.

As this more or less echoes how I feel about myself at the moment, I let it pass. I can't think of anything to add. We know where we stand, more or less. Gynecology isn't rocket science. What good would it do to go over the plan we've agreed on? Nothing's changed since last week. We have less time, is all. Are we going to be parents? Do we want to be? Such are our questions.

"I can come back. I can go with you," I offer.

She studies the floor while her tongue probes her gums and pushes out her thick lower lip, as it always does when she gives something the twice-over.

"No. Go help your godfather." Then she asks: "Does this mean you do 10th grade all over?"

"No," I assure her.

"What about finals?"

"Post said I can still take them."

She plucks a guitar string. Rene sings, plays lead guitar and piano, and has a handle on several brass instruments. "You talk to Astro yet?"

"Not yet."

"You have to. You know that." Her stare brands me: *Guilty as charged.*

"I know it."

"It was a pretty dumb thing you and Klyt did. What were

you thinking?"

This is an excellent question for which I have no answer. I could say it's the zeitgeist but Rene's no fool. Or I could point out it was Klyt's idea, which is true, but that's no excuse for what happened. I am the author of my fate, sure, but there's a lot of pressure. I stare blankly at her long eyes, her puffy pink mouth.

"You seem to be unusually drawn to minorities, Jonathan," she purses her lips.

It's one of those left field things she's always coming up with, as though I needed proof earth's not her native realm.

"You're going to analyze me now?" (Rene's analyses can be withering—I been there before.) "Anyway, I never noticed. I like whoever interests me. Do you see yourself as a minority?"

"Yes and no." She puts a skinny finger to her nose. A callous marks her hours on guitar.

"What's that mean?" I look at Rene, and it's like someone keeps hitting the refresh button every few seconds. She actually vibrates—her entire body, especially around the fingers, trembles, ever so slightly. Cell phones make her crazy. She registers the signals passing through the air, she says. She can feel the texts and calls zipping by. At the same time, whatever grounds a lightning rod drove through her, down into the earth, deeper than anyone might expect, or hope. You feel this right away.

"You're a typical Sagittarius," she says.

"What's *that* mean?"

"Impulsive. Ready to try new things. Eager to go."

Something crashes to the floor below. Probably just the

resident raccoon foraging through the trash. For a city, Cambridge has a lot of wildlife.

Rene gets up. She pushes the loose black hair out of her eyes. In the fluorescent light, her skin is white as paper. For a second she looks just like Yoko Ono in the poster in Mom's room. Took me six months of stealing glances at her—in US History, by her locker, outside the library, months of baby steps her way at lunch, before we finally wound up sitting next to each other during an assembly and I got the nerve to talk to her.

I think she's coming over to give me a good-bye kiss or at least a hug, so I stand up too. Instead she shakes her head, looks away, that small straight nose pointing her path, and walks slowly for the stairs. "See ya," she says, without looking back, going down.

"Watch out for the raccoon," say I.

* * *

After she leaves, I rock in the dark a while, listening to the mice, the raccoon, and my endlessly chattering brain. Shouts from the house reach in and grab me by the throat. Invisible fingers tighten, squeeze. I remember, years ago, after hours of similar arias punctuated by slamming doors, Mom bundled Asia in scarves and stuffed her into the stroller, then grabbed me by the wrist, whispering: We're done, we're free, we're going home. Liberation was the big theme in our house: someone, somewhere, always needed it. With her tumbleweed hair and wild gaze, she looked like Gene Wilder in one of my favorite movies, *Young Frankenstein*. It was snowing out yet we marched into the blizzard, hatless, and down to Mass Ave where we plunged blindly into the pummeling wind. Umbrellas imploded, cars skidded into the curb, defeated bicyclists got off and walked. A lone, empty bus, headlights on, sat with its engine idling in the middle of an intersection. Grey exhaust plumed into the dithering sky. We got as far as the Arlington line before the snow drifts, banking up to my chest, finally forced us to turn back.

And this was what ten years of marriage did for people? Not exactly a shining way to sell the concept. I mean, I love Rene. We'd talked about going to Montreal for a weekend once school was out. Now, who knows?

The noises of late spring make me think of how little I know about the critter world. I'm a city kid. Except for that camping trip to Vermont with Rene, I've only seen nature in movies. It's true we did once spend a week in the Berkshires so Dad could hear Ozawa's last hurrah with the BSO and hang with Spielberg at the Blantyre (fyi, the room we stayed in had a commode formerly owned by Marilyn Monroe and Joe DiMaggio). After dressing for the show, I sprayed myself with bug juice head to toe. "Nature red in tooth and claw," Dad quipped each time we stepped outside. Neither did we do beaches. Once, driving some poet around the North Shore, Dad looked at the people on the small strip of sand and said: "Took us more than a billion years to work our way out of that mess. What's to see?" Our destinations were always either museums, restaurants, or both. The Louvre, The Rijksmuem, Bilbao, the

Uffizi, the Prado. Bernardin, Bouley's, Café des Artistes. Opera for the middle class, Mom called our fretful evenings of fine food. This year Dadsky had been threatening us with the Hermitage, but Russia's still a bit wild.

Mom's idea of a good time, on the other hand, is visiting disaster areas. She doesn't really notice nature unless it's throwing a fit. I've never seen her feed a bird or work in a garden. But: Hurricane strike? Tsunami devastated your coast? Tornadoes smite the trailer park? Volcanoes, earthquakes, and nuclear accidents all have one thing in common: Mom, who dreams of weekends in Chernobyl, Haiti, Bhopal. If Moses could part the Red Sea, surely Mom can do a little thing—like stop global warming, for instance. Fortunately she's only taken me a couple of times, once to New Orleans, and once, when I wasn't ten, to Manhattan after the big one. Bingo: no more family vacations!

Finally I get up. I survey the studio, taking note of all I'll be leaving behind. There's a box beside the battered Marshall amp with my childhood books and diaries. Kiss it good-bye. A baseball glove from eighth grade—remnant of my efforts to fit in with "my peers." Ciao, glove. I'll never forgive you for missing that ground ball to third. Somewhere in that box is a copy of my one and only novel, which I wrote when I was ten, called *The Fight Between Monsters*. Thought I was writing about vampires, werewolves, Frankenstein—but I'm starting to believe it was about matters closer to home. Farewell, my not-so-darling past. I will return—but I will not be the same. This I know.

* * *

It's late by the time I get back from my mission. Mom glares at me as I slink through the kichen.

I check Asia's room. My sister still sleeps with her arms around a stuffed horse large enough for her to ride. I feel guilty leaving her alone with the Keepers, but she needs to find her own way of coping.

Thanks to her, just by the way, we were, for several weeks, a house divided on the subject of some actress and her husband. The actress was a smart babe, kind of fakey aristo. But she married a Monster-Car-loving shit-kicking biker dick. The subject arose because my little sister loved the actress. Mom said it was tragic that such a smart and gifted woman would want to marry a male bimbo. Dad said it spoke volumes about the values of the American female: she wants to be righteous while getting drilled hard. He said this in front of Asia and me at dinner. Mom then said there was nothing wrong with getting drilled hard now and again. Quoth Dad: "I rest my case." Asia then asked what it meant to get drilled hard. Asia is ten. All three turned to me to cut this Gordian knot. "Google it," I suggested. Then Dad left the table.

I'm in bed, flipping through Comb's book on embouchure, when the door opens and Dad's bulb head lights up the room like a bad dream. I can smell the whiskey (Glenfiddich, single malt). Seeing me where I should be, he slowly shuts the door.

Don't get me wrong; I dig poetry. Really. This year in English we read *Tintern Abbey* which I thought was almost as good as an Alan Alda *Nature* special. Unfortunately, Dad's poems

23

make me think of *Sponge Bob Square Pants.*

But when the house is totally quiet, long after Dad's turned off the set, I open my eyes. Like who can sleep anymore, right? I think about how all these years Dad was Dad and someone else. Was he dreaming about Mr. Right the whole time? Is he sorry he had kids? He's tried having "a conversation" with me for weeks, but I don't want to hear it. I just don't. So what if I don't even know where I'll be living next year, right?

I blame Pablo Neruda. Dad happened to read one of the dude's poems to his students when he was a TA. Mom, who was in that class, was in love with the Chile-man. Hearing his words on Dad's lips ("Body of a woman, white hills, white thighs," blah blah blah) must have confused her. She must have believed Dad thought like that. And I'm sure he did nothing to correct that impression.

To review: I am in my bed in a house in Cambridge in the Commonwealth of Massachusetts, in the good old U.S.A. I'm 5'9", 143 lbs, and growing. I have a girlfriend (preggers, maybe). I play in a band. I own a copy of *Bleach* in mint condition. All these things I do and have: but are they really me? Because I also have these thoughts zipping around my brain like loud red birds, and they're me too. It makes me sick to think about it. Sick enough to sit up. The more I think about it, the more I'm sure I did what I did because my parents wanted me to: they wanted to forget their own problems by focusing on me. Only it didn't work, did it? They still can't focus on me.

I wonder if Rene's awake. If she's thinking about me. Or the maybe kid. Black hair on her naked shoulders—she never wears a nightgown. Chewing on her lower lip. I bet when she wakes up in the middle of the night, she reaches for a book and does extra homework. And if there's some of me inside her? Too much. She, growing another me. An "*us*." To tell you the truth, I want to scream, but don't worry, I won't. It could be worse: I could be morbidly obese. The beating of my heart makes me think of what it means "that one just like it may be growing, this minute inside her." Is that how it goes? The cloning. What comes first: the feet, the head, the body, or the heart? Do we grow from inside out or outside in? I could Google it but that would be like T.M.I.

I try to stand, but immediately feel dizzy, so I lie back down. I think about New York, my godfather, Dad's college pal. Visiting him was like seeing another friend my age who somehow happened to live in a cool place and have a job.

* * *

You are born. You open your eyes for the first time. There it is: the world! Before you know it, your mother's shoving her tit down your throat. You hear your old man's voice screaming *shut up*, and you can't even talk back yet. Your first encounter with the Fascist Bastards who will plague your life. It stays like this, more or less, for a long, long time. Not long enough. One day the tit's snatched away. No can have, no more, find your own. And that's the journey I'm on.

Memoirs of an Anarchist

Memoirs of an Anarchist

1

The next morning I'm sitting in the kitchen, duffel bag at the door. My bus doesn't leave for a while but I'm antsy. Waiting sucks.

"Eat your muffin," Mom says. She's at her computer already. Nervous energy ripples off her like a heat wave. She glances at me, turns away, head sheathed in a hippie babushka. Dad comes in. He looks hung over: eyes bloodshot, forehead damp. Pours himself a cup of coffee. Sits down at the table. Things get very quiet. I stare at the muffin. Suddenly Mom rises without a word and walks out of the room, flip-flops slapping.

Alone with Dad, I keep my eyes on that muffin like it's a crystal ball. Dad slurps his coffee. Pushes back his chair. All through grade school I had stomach-aches. Sometimes I'd throw up after breakfast. I suspect my response was only partly commentary on my educational experience. Dining with Dad is hell.

"You're angry at us, Jonathan. Me. You're especially angry at me. Because you think I'm doing this to you and Asia. You personally. At your age you can't understand. Some things aren't about you."

He puts a palm on his smooth head like he's feeling for lumps. His brows scrunch up like they do when he's serious. Clears his throat. I can tell he feels bad. This should please me

29

but it only makes me feel worse. Everybody seems to feel bad about what they're doing, but does that stop them?

Mom peers in: "You sure you packed everything? Memorial Day weekend's coming up. I'll see you then, Jonathan." She pauses. "I wish you'd let me take you to see Dr. Plovnick." They want me on pills. *In chemistry we swear.* But what I've seen pills do to kids in school, ain't happenin'. No way, mofo. No way.

* * *

Before leaving Cambridge, having gotten exactly nowhere with my Table of Contents, I stand before Dad's study shelves. I need an angle. A way to show Dad just what's what. He thinks he knows, but I know he knows squat. The only people who buy his books are his students, because he makes them. So many books! They're about all Mom and Dad have in common. Okay, music. Literature and music are the only things they can talk about without fighting. When I was a kid, writers were always dropping by the house. I remember Seamus Heaney singing on the stairs. Then the arguments between Mom and Dad got so intense, people stopped coming. Since Mom's breakdown last year, our only visitors have been from her women's group.

I stare at the rows of familiar names: T. S. Eliot, Walt Whitman, Emily Dickinson, Frank O'Hara. No sense writing about people everybody knows. What of the others? I mean, you ever walk into a bookstore? Acres of dead trees. Billions of shiny covers—like everyone on the planet has published a book. I decide to make my own list. Ten—not necessarily the top, or the bottom. Just ten. Okay, maybe twelve. A baker's dozen. Who's counting anyway? Lady Luck will lead me on. Luck, Mom says, is just another word for karma. No accidents. First, I grab my two favorites: *Prison Memoirs of an Anarchist* by Alexander Berkman and *The Wanderer* by Alain-Fournier. For the rest, I close my eyes and reach. *The Poetry of Richard Lovelace*. Bingo. I snatch a few more and bury them in my backpack. Heavy bastards. So I pull out my iPad and jot down names instead.

* * *

After Rene left last night, I decided I really should see Astro and apologize. What Klyt and I did was so stupid I can't even tell you about it yet. As I said, he lives in "the projects" outside Central Square—a city block of two-story brick buildings around a narrow strip of green and concrete. Do they call them "projects" because they know nobody would really want to live there, except as an experiment? Don't get me wrong, in the People's Republic of Cambridge they don't allow abandoned buildings, broken windows, or crack vials. There are air conditioners in the living rooms which are all painted a beiger shade of beige. I've never seen a rat menacing the kitchen. Yet there's something so helpless about the place, even in summertime when the babies are out in the yard and the mothers are all smoking and talking, it makes me want to curl up under the stairs and sleep. Going there reminds me Astro has a world of friends and experiences I'll never understand, unless he tells me. But he doesn't like to talk about his family much.

When I arrive, his mother is sitting on the stoop in a violet nightgown, smoking. Ever since Astro's older brother Macro was killed, she's been getting weirder. Astro says she often wanders to the variety store on the corner in her pajamas. She nods at me and moves her long skinny legs out of the way.

Between you and me, my mother loves Astro. She says it's still tough for black and white people in Boston to stay friends. I have no idea if this is true but she's told me some stories. I know all about Judge Garrity, Louise Day Hicks, busing, and the riots at South Boston High. More good old days.

Inside, his brothers and sisters spill around the house like pod creatures, hitting a wall, scattering, regrouping. Seeing me, they stop a moment.

"It's Jon-Jon," shouts Beulah, age four.

"He's in there," Simon says, pointing to one of two bedrooms down the hall.

I knock on the door. No answer. Not even the holy holler of the P-Funk he hides in when he's down. I nudge the door anyway.

Immediately I trip over a bed. Five crowd the room like a barracks. Astro's curled in the corner near the window. The shades are up and the same damn moon that's followed me everywhere for years fills the room.

"Yo," I say.

Silence. This is turning out to be the night of the silent

friends.

"Look man, speaking for Klyt and myself, I'm sorry. We're assholes. I admit it. We fucked up," I say, meaning it.

Outside, Beulah is singing a Miley Cyrus song.

I stare at his motionless small silhouette a while. The air smells weirdly of patchouli. Astro, who taught me so much: preemptive whacking off before a hook up, how to get immediate attention in the *ER* (tell them you're uploading to YouTube), what to say to a cop who's harassing you (*my cousin, Barack Obama*—which works better in some cases than others).

I don't know what else to add.

"Old man's shipping me out tomorrow," I tell him. "Remember the Virgins. Family, man." (At which point Astro turns to me and rolls his eyes, but I ignore this.)

"We need y-o-u, man," I jab a pinkie and index finger in his direction. "Okay? I gotta get home."

He says nothing, intent on staring down the streetlamp. He'd been having such a good year, what with Obama showing black folk how to kick white butt, until his brother's death, for which sacrifice his mother got a flag, his dog tag, and a round of taps.

Astro's eyes shine. Outside, someone's shooting firecrackers. Followed by a siren, a shout.

Finally, he speaks: "You are one clueless white motherfucker."

I exhale. It's a judgment I can get behind myself. Unable to hold his stare, I turn away. I feel like shit, but I don't know what else to say. This time I'm the one who leaves without looking back.

On my way home, after failing with Astro, I check the school parking lot where our drummer, Klyt, sometimes hangs with his skater pals. And there he is, solemn as a gunslinger blowing smoke at the night, slumped against a lone car, skateboard at his feet, watching some dude air over an old dog who lies there, tongue out, one eye open. Klyt's shorts are baggy enough to hide a small animal and his black woolen cap is topped with a purple pom-pom.

It's getting cold. I zip my hoodie up. When he sees me, Klyt (real name, Clyde) grunts:

"Yo, Fruit Boots."

Klyt's small and wiry but even so, you look at him, you think *madman*, think *angry lizard*, think *run*. His eyes, set wide apart, are so brown they merge with his pupils, and his nose looks like the business end of a hammer. His father works in a garage near Central Square. His mother's a skinny woman who organizes Athena parties around town. For years we've been begging for an invite. Klyt suspects all the adopted Chinese girls in our school are spies who'll one day flock back to the motherland. Rene likes him even though he's slightly racist and obsessed with military stuff. He's determined to be a warrior but there's a wrinkle: he loves metal of every shade and hue, and the collision of these passions leaves him even angrier than me. Klyt, however, favors extreme industrial, worshipping at the feet of Treponem Pal, Rammstein, Tattoo of Pain, Snake River Conspiracy, etc. I wonder what will become of this band of ours. He's gotten us in deep shit before, like the time we walked into the Tedeschi and he ran out with a pack of slim jims. I had to persuade the cop I didn't know the kid, we just happened to enter at the same time. This latest disaster, for which we were both suspended, began as a debate about whether water-boarding really was torture. It stewed for weeks as jokes and jabs, until we had to know.

When I walk over to him, he points at the skater who is positioning himself for his next run, then leans toward me, his breath peppery and warm: "It's Tsar. Remember?"

"I thought Tsar was like in jail," I say, heart beating faster with each breath as the drama about to explode before us envelops the crowd. Tsar: golden-gloves tough, his younger brother wrestled on the team along with Klyt, who said he was really good.

"Maybe he broke out," Klyt shrugs.

We say not a word about our own "crime." The possibility that Tsar is also an escaped con thrills me. He's no man's bitch and just the kind of guy I need to know. *We the enemy.*

Unfortunately, it's late and I've got to get ready for tomorrow.

"You leavin'?" Klyt asks.

Three kids have laid their bodies down beside the dog to create more of an obstacle. I recognize the chunky blond as Debbie LeRoux from US History. Everyone's eyes are on the skater.

I nod, squinting at Tsar as he gathers speed and goes airborne, goofyfoot and soaring above the trembling flesh. He hits the sidewalk with a clang but, miraculously, stays on. The crowd goes wild: hoots, yelps, whistles, and the rabid stomping of cleated feet. Klyt just snorts and chucks his cig, adding: "You owe us a song, dude."

"Later," I touch two fingers to my forehead and race off.

A block from our house, I finally slow down. My feet get heavy. I don't really want to go in. I stop dead still and listen to the crickets. And, I swear, an owl in some far off tree. Sure wish I knew what it's saying.

2

All the way to South Station, we say not a word. Dad locks his eyes on the road like Mem Drive was the Indy 500. Crossing the Charles, I think about sitting in Dr. Post's office last week, listening to him explain to Dad why he had to suspend me. The school is supposed to be really liberal—but he couldn't let this pass. You could see right away he hated himself for what he was doing. But he hated me even worse for making him do it. He coughed, scratched at his desk with a fingernail, and told Dad about the website I put up. I didn't blame him, really. He was just "doing his job." Besides, I wanted to say to him, Don't you remember, Dr. Post? Don't you remember that sophomore year blows, universally, and that junior year is even worse? Everyone on the planet knows this. Absolutely everyone. Naturally I said nothing. At heart, I'm a chicken-shit.

And this is what scares me. In addition to everything else.

Dad kept glancing over at me like he couldn't believe I would do this to him. Like I did it to *him*. Well, maybe I did. Maybe Klyt and I did what we did to Astro just to show him that you never know what's around the next corner, cause that's life.

At the station, he's about to deliver another speech until I cut him off: "Skip it, Al. I'll call you when I get there." (Albert is his middle name, which he hates.) I grab my duffle and jump out. I don't look over my shoulder until I'm inside. When I do turn, he's still sitting there, which surprises me. Why doesn't he just take off? I know I would, if I had a car. When a homeless man pushing a shopping cart filled with plastic bottles approaches, he drives away.

There's already a line at the gate. Families speaking Spanish; college girls slipping off for action in the city; a few kids my age staring at their sneakers, trying to look invisible. There's even a Chinese couple too canny for the Fung Wah bus. Mom wanted to get me priority seating, but I refused. Do that and you stand in a separate line, beside a frugal nurse from Malden on a tear, and when you board, before everyone else, the others glare at you like you're Kate Winslet sashaying onto the Titanic. No thanks.

The crowd's growing restless when the driver—who's been smoking on the other side of the door—finally decides to let us on. It amazes me they never check your luggage like they do at airports. At least half of us here look like terrorists. A missed opportunity, for both sides.

By the time I get on, three seats remain. Who's least likely to want to share his grim life story with me? My candidate: a short-haired college girl in a crimson sweatshirt whose backpack, napping in the window seat, hasn't paid full fare. She's buried her nose in a book: *Preliminary Materials for a Theory of the Young Girl.* I can tell she wants to chat about as much as I do. Poor kid: she was just beginning to relax, spread out, enjoy the ride, when she saw *me.* Quickly scanned the bus to check my options. What about the seat behind her, next to the kid on the phone? Yes, it's across from the john—how convenient! No risky schlepping back and forth along a vehicle careening madly down the interstate! I feel her willing me to walk on by.

"Excuse me, that seat taken?" I ask, trying to make my voice sound deep, slightly intimidating. She flashes me a look like I tried copping a feel.

"Can you help me put it up?" she glances at her back-pack tenderly as though it were her child. And by help, she means: will you do it?

"No problem." Packed with iron, rocks, and the collected works of Kierkegaard. No space above the seat, naturally, so I hike the length of the bus in search of open territory. Finally, two seats back from the driver, above an old lady so tiny she could fit in my pocket, I find my opening. I heave the sucker up, then stumble back, because the driver has pulled out and suddenly we're flying.

I grip the railing for dear life.

By now, the girl has her earbuds snug and is pretending to be asleep, book open in her lap. How well I know the game. I try not to step on her toes getting to my seat.

Out the window, Massachusetts slowly morphs into Connecticut: exit signs for Newton, Worcester, Sturbridge.... When I see the sign for Springfield, I remember the city was founded by ancestors of the writer Thomas Pynchon. In case you were wondering. States make no sense to me. Maybe if they spoke a different language—Connecticutese, a noble, ancient tongue—maybe then. Maybe. I have an uncle in Vermont who refuses to cross the border into New Hampshire because "they're all savages with guns and flannel shirts." Dad's family is like that. Snobby. Dad, for instance, never sees that brother unless he comes to the city. It was Mom who insisted I go to public school. As I said, Rene is always telling me I should stop whining, that I have it good. I'm not whining, I say. I'm trying to tell you something. But it's like nobody can hear me.

Like Peter Lorre said in that super-creepy movie *M,* where he plays a child-killer: "Nobody knows what it's like to be me!"

I take a sidelong glance at my companion, who seems honestly asleep. Her head droops forward to the left. Her breath catches a little: gremlins in her dreams. Girls are my destiny like guys are Dad's. You'd think that after millions of years we'd know all there is to know about each other and could go about our business with the confidence of ants. Instead, it's like we're born new every day and have to start from scratch, proving who we are—to ourselves, first of all.

Somewhere before Hartford, we exit the highway and pull into an Arby's lot. When the lights go on, it's like a fire alarm: the masses rise as one and rush for the exit, racing for the world's last remaining batch of fries. *It's Armageddon.* My traveling companion, needless to say, is among the first ones off.

Alone—except for the old lady curled up in the front like she's dead—I wonder what the boys are doing now. Astro, of course, is in school—unless his mother has asked him to stay home to help out. Klyt's probably at his old man's garage.

I decide to step into the open air. I follow the trail of straws and plastic cups to the edge of the parking lot and light a cig. There's another bus at the MacDonald's across the street. As I watch the passengers getting off, I think: what if they're our doubles heading in the opposite direction, to the homes we've left?

I pull out my phone. Nothing. Nichts. Nada. Nichoho. Rene is clearly pissed. Hasn't answered either my text or my messages. I try again—this way, at least I can make her feel guilty by piling on the missed calls.

"All aboard," the driver shouts. I imagine taking off instead. Hitching a ride for the open road to who knows where....to visit my uncle in San Francisco, maybe. Ohio, the Rockies, the desert, the Plains! Redwood forest, gulfstream waters. All I need's my own Neal Cassady. Now there's a dude who knew how to party. He was Kerouac's pal and Dad knows somebody who knew him. Maybe he even slept with him, because wasn't Cassady bi? There's obviously a side to Dad about which I know less than nothing.

* * *

The driver honks but I ignore him. If I could go anywhere on the planet, where would I go? You really want to know? Mauritius. It's an island east of Africa. And why? Okay. A year before I met Rene, there was this girl who appeared one morning in my homeroom who was from there. She was the sweetest thing. Shy as a kitten. She talked with an accent that made her lips compact into little kisses. She never looked at anyone for more than two seconds. Not even teachers, when they called on her. She answered their questions with her eyes on her desk. Martine. That was her name. And even though I talked to her only once, in the lunch room, when I spilled my milk and it trickled to her side of the table, I was nuts about her. "I'm sorry," I said. My first and only words to her. She looked at me with eyes so blue you could imagine airplanes flying through them. "*C'est ne pas grave*," she replied. "*C'est ne pas grave*"! For the next week I walked the halls cursing myself, replaying her words over and over like a favorite song: "*C'est ne pas grave*," "*C'est ne pas grave*." They speak French there, you see. She was only with us for six months; her mother was a visiting lecturer at the university. Term over, she returned to the other side of the world.

There's something about the way people show up and disappear that's just wrong. Luckily, soon after that, I met Rene.

Rene says I'm a romantic.

* * *

The driver honks three times. I feel everyone's eyes on me. Run, says a voice, run. It's fight or flight, and I say flee. *Run, Toto, run!* Around me, miles of stores: Target, KFC, Staples, Olive Garden. Where is there to go? Admit it, we're trapped.

I drop my cig and slink back on, tail between my legs. The driver glares. The others give me dirty looks. It's like a perp walk.

The whole bus reeks of fries. My seatmate drowns her face in her shake, extra-thick. Like she's ashamed to be seen with me. I step over her and sink down, careful not to brush her extra-thick thighs, and close my eyes. The bus grumbles to a start. I'm just about to put in my earphones, when she turns to me and says:

"Looked like you didn't want to get back on."

Frankly I'm amazed she even noticed I was alive. I'm not sure what to say. She's got to be at least twenty.

"Thought about it," I say to the window.

As we rumble back onto the highway, the whole strange show of America resumes. America! Is there really such a place? According to mom, the whole problem with America is that we think there is. But there's just people—and animals and trees and oceans. And none of them have names, not really, except the ones we give them. I'm not really sure what she means, but Rene insists there's something to it.

"Tough time?" the girl asks.

I face her. She's not really so bad looking, if you spot her some points. Even cracks a little smile, which makes her look nicer still.

For a minute, I consider spilling my guts. Tell all. Like she's my big sister, who knows what girls want. Might ask me to stay with her in New York. Introduce me to her hotter friends, who know the places to go—not that I care. Her hair is shorter than mine. There are traces of acne on her face. People are sometimes nicer than you think, but I'm not ready to start talking, yet. I pull out *Prison Memoirs of an Anarchist*.

"Ah, you know, nothing I can't handle," I shrug.

She understands, and doesn't push. "Okay," she says and returns to her book while I close my eyes and wonder if I just blew it.

Am I being rude? If I don't stop acting like a dick, pretty soon I won't be able to. I look over. She's staring past me, out the window, book in lap.

"Any good?" I ask.

She turns to me, surprised. "It's great. For a French book," she gives a quick smile to see if I get it. I smile back to signal all's copacetic.

"What's it about?" Lame question!

She doesn't wince.

"How everybody's plastic, like a girl discovering make-up and clothes. Because everyone's just trying on new costumes they've been told are cool so that they'll buy them, keep the system rolling. Because that's the point of things."

I nod vigorously.

"What are you reading?" She sounds genuinely curious.

So I tell her about Berkman, the Russian-Jewish anarchist who tried to kill this guy Frick in Pittsburgh because he was ripping off the people. He missed and wound up in prison, where he discovered the people he was trying to save were more complicated than he knew. There's a lot more to it than what I've just said. Berkman reminds me of Mom and her crazy attempts to make the world better.

My neighbor's turn to nod her understanding.

"Whatcha doing in New York?"

I explain about my godfather. When she asks why I'm not in school, I take a deep breath. I decide to trust her.

I tell her everything. Eyes on the seat in front of me, I start with Dad.

She doesn't say anything. Just listens.

"It's tricky," she says. "He'll probably get married and then you'll have to go to the wedding."

"I know it."

Then she adds: "I never go to weddings. They're such bullshit."

Again we're in agreement. Next I tell her about Rene.

"Will she get an abortion?"

"Maybe."

She shuts her eyes, head pushed back into the seat, while the bus barrels down an open stretch, which quickly clogs again. "That's heavy. Tell her I think she *has* to tell her mother. She's gonna need more help than you can give. No offense."

I shake my head. None taken. Finally, I unfold what Klyt and I did to Astro.

The whole time, she's stares at me like I'm the guy who just shot Martin Luther King, Jr. I fear I've made a big mistake, but it's too late. My crimes are out there, and they haunt me. She hates me now. I see it.

"Wow," she says. "That's pretty crazy."

I'm holding my breath again. "I know. I pretty much hate myself."

"And I see why," she says. "I mean, it's mainly all about your dad. Anybody can see that. But you should probably stop reading stuff like this," she says.

"I know," I say. Truth is, I'm hurt she doesn't understand, and that she's blaming it on Berkman. Blame the Jews, why not? One thing for sure, it's not his fault. That ends our conversation, though. She cracks her book, and I pop in my buds.

I open my eyes as we're crossing the bridge. Passing through the Bronx, I feel New York enter my bloodstream like smack. Not that I've ever tried it. But I have it on good report from fellow band members Klyt and Astro, who claim to have snorted some at a party in Lowell. Cars and buildings shoot through your eyes and crowd your head until it bursts and there's no telling you apart from the city because the two of you are one. The streets sing in your veins. This is the shoe-shine, this is the rain. Your heart beats loud, and louder: this is life! This is the world! Welcome! Welcome!

The bus drops me at 28th and 7th. From the cab, I call Serafina to warn her I'm on my way. As we pass the building in front of which John Lennon was shot, I think of Rene walking out the night before. Not exactly impressed with myself. Maybe acting like a dick's genetic, in which case the blame lies elsewhere. Yet, as we pull up at our destination and I exit the cab, I feel my old life burning away. The sun is bright, the people are loud, and I don't have to deal with Mom and Dad for a few weeks.

It's spring, and I am fifteen.

The doorman stands at attention and salutes playfully. I yank the bill of my cap down over my eyes and go in.

Lovelace Does Manhattan

Richard Lovelace, Poet, 1617-1657

Lovelace Does Manhattan

The biographer Aubrey describes Lovelace as one of the handsomest men in England. So I ask: was Aubrey gay? Another source billed Richard as "the most admirable and beautiful person that ever eye beheld." Two men, just friends? Doesn't smell right. Richard was heir to the great estates of Kent. No proof he palled around with the Archbishop of Canterbury whose primo episcop, St. Augustine, converted King Aethelbert to Christianity in 597. That was when all the trouble began. Don't get me started. It's hard to stay focused on a sunny day.

* * *

Serafina, the live-in nurse, is waiting for me at the elevator, which opens inside the penthouse. *"Bom dia*, Jonatan, Welcome to *Novo York*," she says, stepping back to look me over. "You got to eat, boy," she concludes, shaking her head. Which is funny because I have the munchies all the time. Hyper metabolism. Excellent weed.

Serafina looks like a female wrestler. Big shoulders, arms and thighs like hydrants. But her flower-printed dress, open at the neck, tight around the waist, highlights her evolved upper being. A large gold cross calls attention to the hazards of the bazaar below. You know there's something wrong with me, because I think she's hot. "Put your bag here for now, *meu amor*. That all you got? Young man, you travelin' light. Must be very smart."

"This duffle, phone, and iPad hold all the megabits of life I need," I say, trying to sound humbled by the compliment.

"Nice you stay with *Senhor* Henry." Her voice is lower than most men's. "You good boy. He appreciates. It's hard on him." Her smile widens. Her hands flutter about like they have minds of their own. Tornadoes of possibility whirl around her. Like we were destined to meet.

She leads me to him: Henry Pontopiddan, a.k.a. my godfather.

Frankly, I feel lucky to have one. Not a lot of people do these days. Mom says he was kind of famous once for defending radical types. Hunched in a wheelchair, in the wide-open living room, he's wrapped in a blue silk robe. He also wears a tweed cap I'd never seen him in before. And red Nikes.

He recognizes me. I wait for him to say something. He stares at me like I'm a stoplight. Like he's puzzled by what's going down, and wants an explanation. But I don't have one.

Now he's as peppy as a paperweight, but I remember him making jokes and pinching his girlfriend's ass one Thanksgiving when what we needed most at our table was ass-pinching. He saved us that day. Wasn't the first time—and hardly the last. Could talk an ear off an elephant once. Henry, who was Dad's grad school roomie, told fantastic tales about clients who murdered their mothers, or ran off with millions, or woke up in bed with a circus animal. Always had a fresh babe on his arm, decked out so as to boil your eyes. They would have been less conspicuous if they'd been naked.

He's the only one of Dad's friends I like.

"Jonathan," he says, speaking so slowly my name sounds like a chant. "You see before you what was once a man." His head drops forward theatrically. Still a fine-looking gentleman. Too bad his arms spaz out. He has some control, but Serafina says it's unpredictable. Strokes are like that, apparently.

"Hi GF," I say. "I'm sorry this happened to you." Why's it so hard to talk to sick people? It's like you have to pretend they're not even sick. Even as you tell them how good they look and how sorry you are, you almost never are because you're so damned sure nothing terrible could ever happen to you.

I've done my time with sick folk. When my grandfather was dying—Dad's dad—Mom kept having to remind Dad to visit him in the hospital. But Dad was always busy. When he did go, he took me along for protection. "You look good," he'd say to the old man lying motionless on the hospital bed like a corpse. Dad slings the baloney like a pro. Gramps was so skinny you could practically touch his heart. He wasn't a very nice guy, Dad's dad. Before he got sick he was always telling everyone what to do. He was never mean to me but he was always mocking Dad. He thought being a poet was stupid. So I could see why, after ten minutes, Dad would say he had to go to the office. He'd leave me there alone with Gramps and come back hours later. I didn't mind, so long as I had my iPod. It's not like it was a ton of work. Gramps mostly slept, mouth open. I wanted to shut it for him but was afraid he might choke. Every once in a while he'd wake up, look at me, and shut his eyes again. Like he hoped to open them on someone else. Someone more like Bar Refaeli, maybe.

Henry blinks. His eyes are learning to speak.

An incoming text buzzes my thigh. My little drummer-boy, Klyt. *Dude!* I snort at the cell.

"I show you your room," Serafina says brightly.

* * *

FYI: This may be the greatest apartment on the planet. It's huge. Fenway Park meets musical cancer ward. Henry's a collector. Collects a lot of things, including wounded musical instruments. In the living room alone there's a lipless Steinway, a bullet-riddled cello, and one tortured sax that looks like a giant hunchbacked caterpillar. Many were gifts from clients whose asses—or assets—he'd saved.

Serafina shows me to my crib. "Excuse these," she says. "His mails," she gestures at the boxes overflowing with envelopes. "You need, you call," she says on her way out.

"Thanks."

As I don't have anything to unpack, really, I peer into the box: magazines, bills, maybe even letters. Then I step out to see what's changed since the last time I was here a year ago.

Whenever things between them got so bad they didn't want any witnesses, my parents shipped me south. Mercifully, GF always acted like he loved nothing better than to diddle the day away in the company of a kid. He took me everywhere: restaurants, parties, the Met, the Museum of Natural History, the Sex Museum in the Village. Even the courtroom. He talked to me like my opinion mattered. Even when I was a little kid, he acted like I was a grown-up. His stories showed me that, no matter how normal things might look, below the surface of life runs a river of crazy which can, at any moment, flood the banks. Like I said, he used to do mostly mom-style political stuff. Later, though, he turned to criminals and celebs, because, he explained to me, New York ain't cheap. I remember the summer I was twelve—he was in the middle of a murder trail. His client was accused of killing his Chinese wife with a machete. GF rarely talked about his cases but this one he couldn't shut up about. He didn't like this client, who made creepy jokes about chop suey wifey. Maybe I remember this one especially because of Rene. Finally I asked why he was trying to save the dick. "Because he asked for help," GF explained. He was always doing that, helping someone out, including people he hated. Even now he's teaching me. I feel it. Then the GF added: "And because he's my neighbor."

I walk down the hall. It turns. Doors open. It goes on. More doors. Walls lined with prints by…looks like P-i-r-a-n-e-s-i? I stare at the Pantheon, which I remember first from fifth-grade mythology. Near the end of the hall is a room that's always locked. Henry claims it's where he keeps his guns. I've never been inside. I try the knob. Once. Twice. I've always wondered about it—is it in fact something else? An S & M chamber maybe? Or a lab where he brews crystal-meth? GF, breaking from bad to worse. Ever notice how many secrets old people have? It's like they're all spies or something. That lock's days are numbered.

At the end of the hall, there's a room with a stationary bike and a treadmill, but who needs them? Where's the cab to take me back to the living room? I fire a jay and calm descends.

Missing are any chairs in which a human being might want to sit. Aside from the white leather couch, everything's armless eggshells and hard cubes. Maybe the designer was into Lego. A balcony, green with potted plants and iron furniture, surrounds us. I step through an open door into the warm, moist, busy air: horns and planes and shouts and a high, whistling breeze. There's a stairway over my shoulder leading to the roof where I discover an outdoor pool beside a monster hot tub. Below, the city unfolds like a giant apartment. Imagine the millions, each in their rooms, getting ready for the evening, powdering their testicles and whatnot, before tumbling into the street to be swept away who knows where.

I watch the sun go down on Jersey. I live for night. In darkness, all things shine. Despite the breeze, I'm sweating. I wipe my face on my shirt and head back in.

Speaking of secrets, I wonder if this is how it starts: Rene and me. Because now we have one of our own. Felt cool, at first, knowing something no one else did—grown up and real. Like this is what they don't tell you about. The stuff you can't see. For a while, you feel it's the two of you against the world, and you of course are bound to win. After a time, it starts to change. Becomes more like a fungus festering inside you, expanding in the dark, inch by inch, feeding on your organs, until eventually it's coming out of your ears and your mouth, and pretty soon it's taken over. Suddenly, you're not you: you're the fungus.

Which is what I think happened to Dad.

Inside, I count two giant plasma TVs, one in the living room and one in GF's bedroom, but there are smaller ones everywhere else—the kitchen, my bedroom, the bathrooms. Funny how old-fashioned they seem, like that rotary phone on display at school. And instruments, everywhere: a piccolo trumpet sans valves, a bassoon that looks like it was last used as a bazooka, a French horn with a bell battered as a crumpled glove.

"Chicken hearts in the fridge," Serafina says. Chicken hearts? "A little fried yucca, too, sweetheart," she nods. "If you wants a snack before dinner."

"I'll wait," I say. I look at her and wonder: what if I was to tell her about my little situation? She might have some ideas. One good idea is all I need.

"Can I help?" she asks. I've been staring.

"I'm okay," I mumble.

Back in my room, I collapse on the bed. Big things are going to happen here, I know it. After a few minutes, I open the Table of Contents on my iPad and make some notes:

The poet Lovelace likely had a big schlong. This is just a guess. After his release, he supported the Royalist cause and fought at Dunkirk, which later became the site of a notorious battle where a shitload of people died. This is because of bad karma accrued earlier. Research is so complicated, especially with all the new information pouring in daily.

* * *

That night I eat dinner with my hosts. The three of us sit at the glass table below the creepy chandelier that looks like a daddy long legs of blown glass, with bulbs for feet. GF can move his arms better than I thought, but his legs are folded ties.

Serafina, who has her own room near the kitchen, washes, dresses, and feeds him. I wonder if she washes him…everywhere. Does it embarrass her? Does she discuss her patients' things with other nurses? Do they ever imagine doing it with their patients? I'd love to hear the conversations around her dinner table. Does she even have family? When does she see them? Her eyes always look like she's about to fall asleep, except the rest of her is shedding all this heat like a little portable stove. She's feeding him so patiently, it kills me. Corn keeps rolling off the fork, black bean soup dribbles down his chin. Honestly, no offense, it's gross.

Henry asks: "How's your mother holding up?" The voice, which once boomed out like every place was court, is soft.

I pause before answering. I want to say she's insane. I want to tell him they're both crazy. I want to tell him Asia cries herself to sleep every night. But nothing comes out. I shrug.

He can see I'm struggling here. "Mmm," he says. "Yes. I see." Then. "Don't worry. My friend. It will. Be Ok."

When he's done it's like he just delivered the Gettysburg address. He closes his eyes.

Seeing how awkward things have quickly gotten, Serafina asks me why I was kicked out of school. I make up a story about getting into a fight with the captain of the football team. The tale makes me sound both heroic and slightly dangerous. I keep glancing at Henry. I'm sure Dad told him everything, but I'm counting on him to go along. It's not like I want to lie, but I can't help it: sometimes an idea gets a hold of me and I have to see how it sounds.

"What about your cases, GF? Did you have to quit?"

"He still sharp," Serafina hurries to defend him. "You got a lotta people waiting on you, Mr. P. Lotta mail. People still calls." She leans toward him and runs her finger through his hair. His nose is practically buried in her chest. She kisses his forehead and looks at me as though to make sure I understand just what she's telling me here.

"Partner," he pipes up. For a minute I think he means Serafina. I nod and turn to my plate so as not to see the food dribbling from his mouth. The trip from plate to fork to mouth takes days. I have more questions but the telephone rings and Serafina rises to answer it.

"Your mother," she says, standing in the doorway, leaning forward enough to make not peering down her blouse offensive. "She want to be sure you really here." I shrug my shoulders, roll my eyes.

Dinner over, may I be excused?

I go to the window. So Serafina's more than just his nurse. That's not really a surprise. Maybe they were together even before his stroke—nobody tells me anything, after all. Outside, the lights have come on and I feel an intense desire to go down to the street and meet everyone. Stand on the corner shaking people's hands like I'm a politician or something. "Mind if I listen to some music?" I ask.

"Have a good time," Serafina urges.

Dre's on, I drop down on the white couch while she parks Henry beside me and clears the dishes.

He looks my way and winks. He's got that slightly pissy smell sick old people have. My grandfather smelled like that all the time. Like he'd just put on his favorite cologne: *Piss.*

I crank the volume up until the world goes away. Peace at last. For those who favor metal over hardcore, let me remind you: it all comes out of Punk's black rubberware. No. Scratch that. The records show: Chuck Berry banged rock and roll into being. *He* is Iggy's real pop. One day soon I'm gonna grab my cornet and blow: a note that's sure to burst the skulls of even the dead.

I'm deep in the groove when, around eight, a man comes by to help Serafina put Henry to bed. Serafina can get him up in the morning, but by evening she's tired and worries about dropping him. "I'm glad you're here," he says to me before being wheeled out. It just about does him in.

Werner, the aide, is tall and skinny and wears a muscle shirt under his black leather vest, a skull-tipped silver stud piercing his lower lip. He too never speaks. He's like those gold-sprayed living sculptures doing the Statue of Liberty etc. Sees me, grunts: *hunh. Hunh* back at you, dude. I suspect he isn't American either.

GF used to let me stay up late so we could watch old movies together on Nick at Night. Afterwards, he'd ask me what I thought of the acting, the story, the dialogue. Hard to say, since most of the time I was focused on some starlets' tits. He made me stretch. Now, I stand in the door of his room to see him laid out under hyper-crisp white sheets, watching Animal Planet with his eyes closed. Tube drones all night.

* * *

Later that evening, I step out onto the balcony again. In the gap between towers, I glimpse lights wiggling over the Kate Hudson River, old Jersey blinking beyond. Poor Jersey. Something about the state makes me pity it. Walking to the other side of the building, I watch the traffic winding in and out of Central Park. So many cars, lights, windows—and me. Is it really possible that, to someone else, I'm a stick figure, a cipher, a comma, a speck—or not even there at all? It feels so wrong. *It's me!* I want to shout. *I'm here! Don't shoot!*

Sometimes I crack myself up.

The May breeze keeps all mellow. I close my eyes and imagine Rene and me inside a custom-made rocket heading for M-82, the nearby galaxy from which scientists have been receiving radio signals unlike anything they've ever seen. Alone, we'd start a new world. Get it right. My only requirement for a galaxy is good wireless.

I take out my cell and call home, deliberately dialing the landline no one ever answers. No one does and I leave what I hope's a funny message for Asia, hi to Mom and Dad, while watching a helicopter land on a nearby building. Air drums like war, forcing me to shout into the phone. You'd think by now they'd have a better muffler.

Hearing Asia's voice on the answering machine reminds me wars are liable to break out just about anywhere. My sister took our parents' fighting hard. One night some years ago, while we still shared a room in the apartment in Medford, their shouts woke us. "You never called...." "The place was a...." "How can you..." It took only a few words for me to recognize if this was Argument #1, #6, #17, or #23: money (lack of), work (too much), politics (insane or insaner), or the shape of the moon on a clear night. I was becoming convinced of invisible forces besieging the world of grown-ups. They—we—were under attack—but by what? Normally Asia and I would tell each other stories to take our minds off what we couldn't change. This time, instead of talking, Asia began to gasp. She couldn't breathe. I called for Mom, who quickly called an ambulance. We spent the better part of the next year going back and forth to Children's Hospital. Doctors called it *pericarditis*: water around the heart. Like all the tears she needed to release got stuck inside. Mom and Dad freaked and, for a while there was peace.

It didn't last.

Looking at the building where the helicopter landed, I'm thinking binoculars when a voice says: "Got a smoke?"

I whirl around. Leaning against the wall overlooking Central Park stands a big dude wearing a dark suit. His hair's banded in a pony tail. His head, framed by the Park and uptown lights, is large, New York-sized, and his smile shows teeth.

"Sorry, man," I shrug.

"Oh. You're a kid. Apologies."

This whole bit of being a kid's beginning to drive me crazy. I think of blurting out: I'm practically a father, asshole! But I don't.

"You kin to Henry?" he asks.

"Sort of. How'd you know?"

"You're on our balcony, old man. Didn't think Henry had people. Never saw him with anyone except his girls. Terrible what happened. If it can happen to Henry, everyone's vulnerable. You his nephew or something?"

I explain about Dad and the GF.

"Oh, I know who you are. You're Madeline's kid," he says, raising his collar against the breeze.

Hearing my mother's name in a stranger's mouth is creepy.

"How do you know that?"

"Henry talked a lot about her. But then, Henry talked about everybody. One of the great talkers, you know?" The Suit looks over his shoulder at the street from which a shout drifts up like it was miles away. It's always weird when someone you don't know knows stuff about you. Immediately I think *NSA!* But I have no interest in mapping my parents' world, which has already swallowed my whole life, so I change the subject. When I ask what *he's* doing here, he tells me he lives on the other side of the building. He shares the roof-top deck with two other neighbors.

He asks how old I am.

"I wouldn't have done it at your age," he says quietly. "Taken care of an old man. Not so old, really. My age. At your age, life was soccer and chicks. My age, you start asking: Will I feel I've lived if I die without ever having owned a monkey?"

His eyes widen like he's wowed by his own crazy. He rocks back and forth on his heels. "Don't mind me, kid. I'm in a funny place." He puts his hands on the wall and leans over, as if to get a closer look at the pigeons on the ledge below. The wind's sharp and I'm getting cold.

"You thinking of jumping?" I ask on a hunch.

"Nice meeting you, kid," he replies without turning around. Then he pushes off the wall and walks in the direction of the water tower.

The helicopter next door rises up and I and everything around me—the birds, the buildings, the streets, even the moon—are pulled into the whirl of its blades.

* * *

Back to poore Richard. Night is racing by; information streams in like starlight. But the bio screams for an update. Wonder if anyone will notice:

When he's two, the Pilgrims land at Plymouth Rock. In 1629, Charles the I dissolves Parliament and rules personally, from his own treasury. Thirty-one years after his death, Parliament establishes the *Act of Habeas Corpus*, which has zero to do with sex with the dead, despite my little sister's claims. Where might she have heard that? Fourth grade? In any case, more than three centuries later, our former president abolishes it.

Whenever I write a sentence I like, I get so excited, I have to stop and pace. I stomp up and down the room like it's a cage. What's Asia up to, I wonder. Asleep, I hope. Recently she asked me about sexting. She said she and her friends argued whether or not it was legal. I decided then and there I would never have children. Rene will have to abort. As though she feels my thoughts (and maybe she does), the phone rings.

"How is he?" Rene asks.

I imagine her naked in her bed under the poster of Neko Case, blanket pulled to her neck, because she's always cold, like mom.

"Okay, I guess. Can't talk much. And he's stuck in a wheel chair. But he's got Serafina."

I poke around the box of mail. Most of it looks like junk. But not all. Serafina said someone from his office stops by weekly to sort through it.

"Who's Serafina?"

I pull out a catalogue: *Hammacher Schlemmer.* On the back cover there's a picture of a submarine you can buy for just seven mill. Place your orders early. Never know.

"His nurse. She's from Brazil. I think she may also be his mistress."

"Typical," Rene replies. I drop the catalogue back in the box and wait for her to mention the possible impossible kid.

The reason we're still not sure is because she's tried two fail-proof tests. One came back positive, the other negative.

The first almost gave us heart attacks; the second, hope.

"I miss you," she says.

To which I say nothing. I know I should tell her I miss her too but for some reason the words won't come. Even though I do miss her. My mind goes blank. "I gotta work on my essay," I finally say. She hangs up.

In bed, I alternate between researching my subject and making notes on the past week:

*fought with girlfriend
*tried making up with band-mate
*lied to both parents, and got away with it, naturally
*met Serafina, GF's mistress-nurse
*"enjoyed" a gross dinner with the GF
*talked to a future suicide
*am watching the greatest movie ever made: Grand Illusion by Jean Renoir. (This one is not debatable.)

To conclude:

Lovelace is eventually thrown into Abu Ghraib, where he writes his most famous poem, *To Althea in Prison*. It's possible he is water-boarded by some ancestor of the Bush clan, which famously traces its roots to Merrey Olde Englande. Lovelace wrote: "Stone walls do not a prison make/Nor iron bars a cage./Minds innocent and quiet take/That for an hermitage." Think about it: it's the perfect cure for Fascist Bastard syndrome. Maybe the only one around. The babe he called Lucasta, whose real name was Lucy Sacheverell, decided he was dead and married someone else. This is the kind of luck poets used to have, before tenure—says Dad. Luckily, Dad has tenure. Otherwise, Mom said, he could never afford the divorce. T'ain't easy being the son of a poet. Or, as Lovelace himself put it, "Poets and bravos leave Punks to their Mothers." Who knows what he meant?

Stone walls most certainly do prisons make—at least the ones I've seen. One year Mom volunteered to teach journaling at a women's "correctional facility," and when she wasn't able to get a babysitter, she took me with her. Alone in the car, I'd watch her walk through the doors and wonder if she would ever reemerge. Sitting in the front seat of the Subaru, I'd study the women being led in, cuffed and grim-faced, flanked by some pretty brutal-looking babes. Sometimes I imagined Mom being attacked by the prisoners; other times, it was the guards. As this was at the height of the Parent Wars, I also imagined her asking to be kept in, rescued from her life with Dad. I saw myself sitting in the car for days, waiting, growing thinner and thinner, scratching at the window as strangers passed, turning away or oblivious, until I disappeared altogether, like fog on glass.

Lovelace was right. Stone walls are not the *only* way to build a prison.

* * *

That night, I dream I'm back on the roof.

"You spend far too much time on the roofs of luxury buildings, young man," says a familiar voice. Suit's wearing the same threads he had on earlier. He probes his belly with the tips of three fingers like he's hosting someone inside. His left foot drums a beat. His skin's banana-yellow. Blue and red fish float through the sky.

Out of nowhere, I ask: "What about my mother?"

In my dream I'm feeling this panic—I mean, I know I'm dreaming but I can't wake up.

Cackling sounds rise from the streets. Below us, the sidewalk is teeming with worms. "Want to see how the other half of the building lives?" he says.

Next, we're in a room with drawn curtains and dark, modern furniture. The walls are covered with cartoons. I recognize images from *Toy Story*: there's Woody and Buzz Lightyear and Mrs. Potato Head. A life-sized statue of a guilded Buddha, sitting in front of an empty fireplace, coughs.

"Want to see something cool?" He looks both ways, like he fears someone's listening. His bottom left eyelid twitches. The apartment feels cold. "You've never seen anything like it before, and neither has almost anybody else." He sweeps his hands in front of him like he's knocking bottles off a table. Finger to lips: "Wait here a minute."

He returns with a large round silver canister about two feet tall. It's polished so bright I can see the room curving around it. "Come over to the table," he says.

Placing it under the chandelier, he unscrews the lid and reaches in, pulling out a large glass jar. Inside the jar stands a very lifelike doll in a short black dress. Blond and green-eyed, her lipstick looks moist and the earrings glint like real diamonds. The skin on her knees appears scratched and I notice a run in her black stockings. She looks as real as a miniature person. I can almost see her chest swell and fall. Then, out of the blue, the doll steps forward and, splaying both palms against the glass—they arrive with a splat and her palms glow red— begins to speak:

"Where the hell have you been? I've been waiting in the dark like a dummy how long? Think I like standing at attention for days, alone, nowhere to go, nothing to do?"

She slams both palms against the glass again and scowls. Her voice is bright and loud but when I lean in for a closer look, she swivels her head my way and snaps:

"Who the hell are you? If he thinks I'm going to entertain his friends, he doesn't know me! Punk." Then she turns back to Nile, hissing: "You promised you wouldn't show me to anyone again." The look on her face reminds me of Mom in a rage.

"What is it?" I ask.

"It?" The doll screams. "I look like an *it* to you? You're a disgusting kid! You listening to me, Philip Nile?"

"All right, all right, babe," he says. "That's enough."

"Enough?" she shouts. "I'm just getting started."

Nile picks up the jar while the doll cries "Philip, Philip," adding: "I hate you I hate you."

Once he screws the lid of the silver canister back on, we can't hear her anymore.

"What the fuck?" I say.

Then, from nowhere he says: "Henry has his skeletons. I gave them to him, you know."

I wake up thirsty. On my way to the kitchen, I see Serafina at the other end of the hall talking on her cell phone. She cups her hand over her mouth and disappears inside her room.

The oven clock says it's 3 in the morning.

* * *

If any reader still thinks this is going to be a coming of age story, I'd like to say right away: pluck your head from your ass! Surely it's clear by now that nobody comes of age anymore. I mean, seriously—who? Not my parents. Old man's way over fifty and, near as I can tell, clueless. Who? Our presidents? They kill people then brag about it on television. Dr. Post? Everyone knows he's having his way with Mrs. Black, the guidance counselor. So, who? You?

Apologies for the rhetorical question. Sometimes I do that. Because I don't know how else to say what I really want to ask: like, how can these "grown-ups" think it's okay to do what they do to us? Believe me, I know that what they do in other places is much worse. In September 2001, I wasn't even ten. School had just started. We had no homework yet I was already falling behind. But we've been bombing people most of my life because of what happened that day. And that is the world of the grown-ups.

* * *

Eventually Lovelace burns through his inheritance. He becomes "poore in body and purse." He wears rags in place of the suits of spun gold he once favored. He is deserted by his "friends." Do I think Astro and Klyt would help me should I, like Lovelace, one day find myself in Gunpowder Alley? I know perfectly well they would piss on my corpse and steal my weed. In the film version of his life, I see his young self played by Robert Pattinson. His decrepit thirty-year old husk belongs to Jude Law. The poet's brother, Dudley Posthumus Lovelace (I kid you not), finally publishes Richard's first book, which doesn't win any awards. A literary critic observes that, while his two most famous poems deserve their celebrity, about the rest "it can without rancor be said it would be better if they had remained in manuscript and perished ."

When All That Remains

When All That Remains

1

When all that remains of my father is print, I want these words to stand beside his on every library shelf.

My father was born on December 13, 1954, on Irving Street in Cambridge. ee cummings lived a few blocks away half a century earlier—a fact Dad pointed out to anyone in range, as though to prove the area's durable lodestone of poetic grit. Dad's grand-dad, my great-grandfather, who ate a bullet long before I arrived, was a heavy duty cock-meister and...nah, can't do it....As I said, family history isn't my thing.

Let's try this instead:

Not only is Dad a shameless self-Googler, he also makes his students subscribe to his Twitter feed so he can share his latest insights about this week's *New Yorker.* He radiates insane, even violent ambition. He covers the map of my world like an oil spill. There was a time when we used to shower together, wearing swim suits. He'd soap me and I'd soap him until Mom finally made him stop.

Dad is also super-impressed that he teaches at Harvard. Half his sentences begin: "At Harvard, we..." Amazingly, the words work weird magic. People fall under his spell like he was Dumbledore. Mom, on the other hand, claims Harvard has only two goals: teaching money to replicate itself, and perpetuating the cult of the bow-tie. She says the school's been morally bankrupted by fat fart economists whose contribution to higher education has been to build new buildings inspired by the work of the late Albert Speer.

* * *

Needless to say, like everyone my age, I think about killing myself all the time. Not all the time. Now and again. The rest of the time, got Rene on my mind. Go figure.

* * *

After two hours of concentrated work, this is what I come up with:

Lydia Maria Child, Novelist and Abolitionist, 1802-1880

Grew up only a few blocks from where we used to live, before Dad's Harvard gig. Her house is now a Thai restaurant with a big *Grand Opening* sign in the window that's been there for years.

Lydia wrote a poem you probably sang in school: *Over the River and Through the Woods.* Grandfather's house stands, an antebellum Victorian with Ionic columns, on the Mystic River. We studied local architecture in art class. Whenever I needed a break from my keepers, I biked to the river where I once saw three turtles piled on top of each other. A terrapin orgy! See why I hated leaving Medford?

In our new Cambridge house, carpeted stairs led to my room. There my real life began: another world was born. I was six, just starting first grade, and already hating it. Not that the teachers weren't nice—they were. But I never understood why, just because we were a certain age, we had to sit with strangers our size, who weren't always friendly. I learned a lot more lying at home in bed than at school.

Every night, Mom would enter my room, book in hand. She'd sink down on the carpet and read to me. This I loved. Not your Shell Silverstein stuff, either. Articles from *The Nation*; weird bits from *Scientific American*; even select items from *People*. It was white magic, inscrutable as algebra: tornadoes of words signaling the weather of a world beyond my room in which all was possible, and nothing certain.

By this time, Mom had already turned her back on conventional home-making. Then began the days of camping out: sleeping bags, rations. She occasionally shopped for food at the Science Museum, where they had these frozen meals prepared for astronauts. Dad didn't seem to notice. He was busy entering poetry contests. Poets are more competitive than hockey players, always scrambling over thin ice, racing for a prize.

For a time, every evening after dinner, I'd get into my sleeping bag and Mom would appear lugging some major tome—*Das Kapital, The Interpretation of Dreams,* Rimbaud, *The Kreutzer Sonata,* or my favorite, *Prison Memoirs of an Anarchist*—and I would nestle in the twilight of her voice, eyes shut, mind filling with images of textile factories in Manchester or faeries in Ireland, transported inside a bubble hermetically sealed against the rude and bewildering world.

What the hell happens to people when they grow up, is what I wanna know.

* * *

It's late, and even this insomniac city is starting to doze. *Pas moi!* I'm scribbling away like a budding Balzac:

Lydia wrote cookbooks and novels and stood up for the slaves and all that stuff. In 1833, she published *An Appeal in favor of that Class of Americans Called Africans.* She insisted on total emancipation without compensation. It was the first book against slavery published in America. In the old days, literature was a lot more like punk. People were so pissed at her, she had to leave Medford. She moved to liberal Watertown, six miles away. It's not the same as tearing your shirt off, but it's still pretty cool. I am learning a lot. I forget the rest of the story. Somehow she survived to the ripe age of seventy-eight. (Background music: the Wankys.)

Day Two

Day Two

1

A painting of a giant blue square across from the bed where I sleep stares at me when I wake up. I think it may be what gave me that nightmare with the doll.

Rain raps the glass. I run my fingers over the soft sheets, then close them into fists and yank the cotton to my neck. Everything important is happening in my life *right now*. I feel it. I'm trying to keep a grip, but it's not easy. The top of my head wants to explode, heart fly out on tiny wings, body peel off like dirty underwear. What's this about? Rene? Dad? New York?

I reach for the phone and call Rene. To discuss our situation. Our cellular surprise. The very thing I couldn't talk about the other night.

"You think I'd make a good father?"

"No," she says without hesitating. "Anyway, since when did you start caring?"

"Then what's to talk about?" I make a face and give the nosey blue painting the finger.

"Plenty. You're not the only issue here."

"I didn't realize I *was* 'an issue.'"

"The question I have to answer," she says as though to herself, "is whether I'm willing to freak out my parents—either by having the child, or by not having it. The only sure thing is they *will* freak."

I imagine Rene saying this: her small lips thick and soft as jelly sponges trembling a little.

"If there is a child," I add, getting up, rubbing the soles of my feet against the carpet. This is starting to feel like Shroedinger's cat. What if we don't look?

"If there is a child," she confirms.

"When will you know?" Walking toward the chair, I trip over my pants.

"What was that?"

"I tripped on my pants," I say.

"Am I on speaker-phone?" Rene asks.

"Yep."

"That's creepy. Who else is listening?"

"Nobody. I'm in my room."

"It's after one!"

I shrug at the phone.

"I'm seeing the bitch tomorrow, if you want to know," she finally says.

The bitch is code for her gynecologist. Rene thinks she's a fetishist—something to do with a four-color tattoo.

I sink to the bed and stare at my socks. Last week, Mom bought me a new pair—like I needed them. Slipping them on the first time, I noticed I'd forgotten to remove the tag. Turned out my socks have their own website, which I visited. I don't mean for the company that makes them. I mean for this particular pair. Knitted from wool carded by Margaret, I can trace the genealogy of the sheep behind it unto the fifth generation. The site offers a close-up of a ewe with a come-hither gleam in her eye. I now know more about my socks than I do about my mother, father, sister, and friends combined.

"Your mom know you're going?" I ask.

"Don't be ridiculous."

Long pause. I pick up my pants, see a brown streak along the seat (how did that happen? Too young for anal leakage!), toss them aside, find another.

Then she says: "Sometimes it's better to stop a thing quickly than to mess up the lives of untold millions."

I had been praying for this. Yet when she says it I wince at hearing my deepest wish in someone else's mouth.

"How can you talk like this?" I stand in the middle of the room, arms crossed, pants brushing the top of my celebrated sock.

"What do you mean?"

"So cool, so tough," I say.

"This, Jonathan, is a tough situation."

I once asked Rene if she ever thought about her parents back in China. Of course, she said. Do you want to meet them? Unh-unh. I didn't doubt she meant it. Something in the way she said it made me realize how much harder this was than she made it look. I could tell she wasn't happy talking about it. What would you say to them if you saw them again, I asked. Without hesitating, she said: I'd tell them they did the right thing. I can imagine the terrible stuff they had to live with. There were probably days they had to suck stones for dinner. It wasn't personal. Maybe they did it for a little brother they already had. All kinds of reasons. Anyway, they didn't kill me. They could have.

This girl.

"If you had the baby would you leave the country?" I ask.

"You mean, like, go to Switzerland or something? Don't be an idiot. Please try. You know my mom, whatever I decide, she'd want me to do it in a way that I felt comfortable talking about it with her on television. After she's done freaking out."

"What Mothers Know. Public access cable," I say.

"Or Dr. Phil," Rene adds.

Her mother's a semi-retired folkie. Still sings now and again. She's also an ex-almost-born-again. The cross Rene wears comes from a pilgrimage to Assisi. Rene and I have talked about this a lot. Her father's an accountant who makes stained glass on the side.

"Anyway, wouldn't you need her permission?" I ask. I've heard Mom say how hard it is for a girl to get an abortion these days.

"Score one for the dads," she says. "It's true. That's the way it is in Massachusetts. I could try for a Judicial Bypass, but I don't think so."

"You mean, see a judge? Never," I say, falling back on the bed where I stare at a spider mapping the ceiling.

"Really, my last question, and it's not terribly important if you think about it, is you."

The spider drops on a thread. He's right above me, like a sword.

Long silence. I have a lot to consider. As I've already been thrown out of school, I suppose I could get a full-time job. In a city of more than eight million, there's gotta be room for one more; surely there's a job out there I can do. On the other hand, maybe I should just bail while there's still time—before any definite information, yes or no, can color my decision. I roll out of the spider's range.

"I'll figure it out," I shrug.

I look at the clarinet on the dresser, below the gilded mirror. I could sell the instruments on e-bay. Who would notice? Or maybe I'll write a hit song. Been known to happen.

"Oh, Jonathan, I just know you will."

After a few more minutes of this, I give up. We agree to talk in a few days. If she weren't so pretty, would I bother? But she is. So pretty, I feel my heart spreading across the globe faster than a computer virus from China. Soon it will cover the world.

I close my eyes and think about the time we made out in the back row of Memorial Hall where we'd snuck in during some crazy-ass violin concert. Or the time Rene accepted Klyt's challenge and danced with him in the Garage outside Newbury Comics. She started slow, as she always does. Before Klyt knew what hit him, he was standing back and watching her click her boot heels in a wild salsa squall, eyes shining, lips wet. Then there was the weekend in a teepee by a pond, behind the house owned by a family friend of her mother's, in Vermont. At night, we built a campfire (Dad would have died) and read aloud from *Wind in the Willows*.

Does sex get better or worse after fifteen? Could this maybe be my peak? When I see how big the whole Lolita thing's become, the ink and web sites it gets, I wonder. And she was what, twelve? Admittedly, I haven't read it yet. Several thoughts about pubescent girls, though: first, their breasts inflate just enough to distinguish them from us. Of course, in some cases, **wow**, but generally speaking. Asia's ten and it's been some years since we bathed together, lovingly wiped by our nomadic mom in a tumultuous tub of holy water.

Rene's turning fifteen soon, but she's not too bad, yet—though, *entre nous*, who would I compare her to? Her breasts are pale velvet, white as coconut flesh. Her nips start off as spider bites, but once I suckle them, they blossom into hardy little buds. Apologies. Dad's the poet in the clan. The involuntary fluttering of muscles, the trembling downy belly, and best of all, the warm and moist unfolding of the parts that have no name—these, I assume, stay the same age to age. But again, how would I know? Aside from the web.

If Rene really is pregnant, then we are, in a whole different way, fucked. But if this is my peak, shouldn't I take full advantage? Isn't it early to be settling down? Like the rabbi said, When if not now, where if not here, who if not I? Me. *Moi.*

I look into the mirror and see hair. A furtive blue gaze. Furtive. Because I love the word. And hunted. A hint of snarl, of wolverine pride, below a sketchy moustache (I plan on not shaving until I finish my assignment—a trick I picked up from Papa—that's Hemingway, not Dad).

Anyway, in New York, no matter what time you wake up, there's action. Yet, for the longest time, I don't leave my room. Coolest thing about the city's the takeout. Serafina offers to make my meals, but before I left Mom suddenly felt bad—we're bonded over Dad—so she slipped me her credit card. I'd hate to compound her guilt by slighting her gift. Here I order bagels and burgers and three cheese omelets, and a guy on a bicycle appears at the door in minutes. Every menu in town is on-line. Luckily my godfather's wireless is unsecured.

2

While waiting, I do a little work. This one's for Rene, who knows almost nothing about her people and culture.

Xu Zhimo, Poet, 1897-1937

He was born in Haining, to well-off parents. His father wanted him to be a businessman, but Zhimo longed to help the poor, so he took up poetry. I have heard this before, from many writers. How do the poor feel about it, I wonder. Are they grateful for the solidarity? Do they even know how much poets love them? When he was fourteen, Xu proclaimed that mankind's greatest mission was to invent wings. In 1918, Zhimo came to the US to study. Three years at Clark and Columbia taught him that we were stupid, materialistic, narrowminded. After hightailing it to Cambridge, England, to complete his education, he happily hurried home.

In China, Zhimo is sometimes called a Miracle Person. Love was his inspiration and he was in love a lot. Not unlike *moi*. Unfortunately, Zhimo's *third* wife was high-end. He worked so hard to keep her in silk that he forgot about the poor, and died in a plane crash in 1937.

* * *

By the time I do leave my room, Serafina's wrapping a pink chiffon scarf around her neck to go out on errands.

"Do you like caring for sick people?"

She shrugs: "When they sweet, like *Senhor* Henry, *querido*."

"Do you have a family?" I ask.

"Ah, querido, they're all in Brazil. I come here to make the money to get them out of the *favela*. Back in an hour," she says as the elevator opens. "Speech therapist be here in twenty minutes. He know what to do."

A few minutes after she leaves, the delivery guy arrives with my order. Weird how they don't ask why your credit card claims your name is Madeline. I am, incidentally, a pretty devastating tipper. 100%. Thanks, Mom. I sit down on the leather couch in the living room, alongside GF in his wheel chair, facing the window, and think about Serafina's family in the slums of Brazil. It seems unfair a person has to abandon her kids and her home to make money. In school they showed a lot of films about people living on like 8 cents a day, and it's tough. But at the moment there's a hot bagel wrapped in foil in my hands, and I must focus.

Now I'm no historian, and lately my taste runs to Japanese anime more than to Gibbon (where, honestly, it never ran), but Dad has always said a writer's proper companions are philosophers and historians and you have to admit it's wild to look back and see how many forces have to come together to create the smallest thing. Take schmearing a bagel, for instance. I'm doing it now. For this to happen you need farms, wheat, ovens, farmers, bakers, inventors, restaurants, delivery guys, bicycles, money. Bagels are the strange fruit of thousands of years of civilization! My fingers are sticky and I'm a little worried about screwing up the iPad, but I refuse to live in fear of technology. The bagel is toasted deep brown and smells great. What did I expect? This is New York; bagels are a native crop. I hold one up to ponder. Such elegance and function: crevices, cupolas, cracks to drown a flea, and in the center, at the heart of everything, if you will, nothing. Nothing at all.

"You like bagels?" I ask the GF, who's staring deep into the world beyond Central Park. I bet he's thinking about all those babes who used to hang all over him. Where are they now?

He nods. "Many pleasures. Many pleasures in the world, Jonathan."

This is what I mean: he doesn't give up. I wonder how I might do something for him. To help me think, I ask if I can plug my iPhone into his Bang and Olufsen.

"Certainly, certainly."

The Subhumans are blasting through the speakers when the speech therapist arrives. Looks like an elf in a grey jacket and tie. Moustache and cuffed pants. He nods approvingly: "Music's just the thing after a stroke." Then he walks over to me and says, kind of formally, "We haven't met. Artie Danton."

We chat. I fill him in on Serafina's whereabouts and ask if the GF will ever be able to walk again.

"Walking, not likely. But his speech is already much better." Then he excuses himself and turns to the GF.

While he works with Henry, I go to my room and scan 4chan for relevant news while catching up with friends in Seattle and Qatar. Like television, life is always on.

3

Forgive me. I've just taken a brief excursus down the seamier back alleys of the web. Places Lovelace never dreamed of. In today's world, knowing yourself means knowing your virtual self too. I won't go into details. All in the name of scholarship.

My research carried me to Versailles and included, unexpectedly, a side trip to the June Cleaver Club which led, with the peculiar inevitability of associative poetry, to the Vulva Massage Club. Who knew? There was much to ponder before getting back on track. More genital therapy is certainly in my future.

But *entre nous,* I believe I'm falling in love with the hostess of the Vulva Massage Club. Even though she's only a virtual girl. What does that mean, *virtual?* Is that like an insult? I see her. Looks more real than most of the babes at school, who will soon be nothing but still-lifes on Facebook. Her name, incidentally, is Bree: a chick of pixels born for love. Tattoo on my palm?

Comes then, after coming, that funny let-down feeling I hate—like, what's it all about? Minutes ago, I was totally focused on the crazy pictures on the screen and in my skull, eyes shut, heart lunatic-slamming, and this energy shooting through my body, launching from my finger tips and toes, aiming in the same direction, a little apocalypse at the core before the universe shut down, ending life as we know it.

Wikipedia calls "ejaculation" a "major landmark" of "puberty" and I aim to leave behind a pyramid or two: Pharaoh

Phallus the Phurst.

But the world doesn't end. Minutes later, you open your eyes and look around, and there's the painting, the boxes, the dresser, your clothes scattered everywhere, and you, suddenly smaller, sadder, and faintly ashamed. Does it ever get any clearer? Does the whole thing ever make sense? Now what?

Bored, I open the top dresser drawer and find it's stuffed with envelopes bundled in batches with rubber bands so brittle, they crumble in my hands. I open the second drawer to find it too jammed front to back. Same with the other drawers. There must be thousands of letters here, scraps and ashes of a dying art. I grab a stack and rifle through them. Addressed to Henry Pontoppidan, they seem to be from the same person, initials MS. The envelopes themselves are strange-looking—small, and blue, the kind in which you put birthday cards. The stack I hold are postmarked January 1977. Most also share the same stamp, which shows a bunch of envelopes scattered on a green blotter above a caption that reads: *Letters mingle souls.* Will they ever say the same about email?

I press the envelope to my nose—sometimes they're spiced with perfume. Nope. I pause to consider whether my strong feelings about Internet privacy extend to this antique technology. I slip a finger in, turn the envelope upside down, and out it flutters, like a butterfly escaping its cocoon, only to land on my palm. Letters live to be read.

Like the envelope, the paper itself is pale blue and small, as is the script covering it. The penmanship's elegant as Arabic— now there's a skill they don't teach anymore. You can tell the person who wrote this was intense. The individual letters themselves are so tightly curled, I have to really focus to read them.

Henry dear,

You are truly the most amazing and much loved. I find it even impossible to attempt to imagine someone more perceptive, brilliant, and lovable than you. That is an unqualified statement, which speaks even more for its truth.

Having just read Roethke's far field, I proceed to the subject it triggers....that of Truro...it is my judgment that we should take the $85 a week cottage. Sandy thinks we should take it, the beaches are a lot more private than at Wellfleet or P-town. We can drive or walk to them. It's nicer to have your own house, anyway.

The other day I visited Reggie who is now washing dishes at the Tavern Club, and continuing his French translations in between bouts with cheese-encrusted tureens. He said poeticizing Prevert is killing him. I promised him when I was in New York I'd get him some other French poetry at Rizzolis where we went last time, remember?

Did you know you really are wonderful when you're drunk? It's a shame you don't remember anything. Just ask me, I remember all of it! Some of it I'll never be able to forget. Tell me, lover, what says the Doctor: have you got 3 more good years left?

Love, m

I put the letter down, go to the window: all the water towers on the roofs below! How does the water get there? Imagine the pipes, the pumps, the linkage, the drills. The little man behind it all. The computer behind the man. Never thought of

Henry the young in love. Pigeons on the ledge stare at me like I'm a loaf of Wonder Bread. I could live my whole life looking out this window.

I return to the pile, fold the paper nearly, slip it back in the envelope, and pull out another, marked in red ink: *Airmail, Special Delivery*—what they did in the days before *Priority* and *Express*. This one's typed, all caps:

HENRY, GOD DAM IT, PUT UP WITH ME FOR A WHILE LONGER YET....TRY TO EXCUSE IF POSSIBLE MY LACK OF MAIL PROLIFANCY, IT IS NOT THAT I FEEL ANY DIFFERENT ESSENTIALLY ABOUT YOU, ONLY A MATTER OF CIRCUMSTANCE, TIME, AND OTHER LOUSEY EXCUSES. IT IS A PAIN TRYING TO ACTUALLY PLAN FOR THE FUTURE YOU KNOW, I AM FACED WITH GUILT EXPECTATIONS, DECISIONS ETC. ALL OF WHICH I WILL FACE OR IGNORE DEPENDING ON THE BEST WAY OUT AT THE MOMENT...DON'T CALL ME IF YOU CAN RESIST, I MISS YOU AND THE DESIRE TO ESCAPE THE WHOLE FUCKING MESS OF LIFE BECOMES OVERWHELMING WHEN I SPEAK TO YOU ON THE PHONE, I PIN MY HOPES ON THE SHORE AND WHICH WILL BE SUCH A SUCCES FOR THE TWO OF US WHEN WE CAN FINALLY TALK EVERYTHING OVER AND EXHAUST THEM WITHOUT THE RESTRAINTS OF MONEY PARENTS FEAR ETC. PLEASE DO NOT BECOME DEPRESSED YOU WOULD NOT BELIEVE HOW DETACHED I HAVE BECOME ABOUT MOST OF MY POSSESSIONS AS IF RIDDING MYSELF OF MATERIAL THINGS COULD RID ME OF MENTAL PROBLEMS

HOWEVER IT WORKS TO SOME DEGREE, MY HATS ARE NOT INCLUDED IN THINGS I COULD GET RID OF THOUGH I DID GIVE ONE TO MY SISTER. I SHALL SOON BE NINETEEN MY LOVE, AN OLD LADY ALMOST AH HENRY, TRY TO REMAIN AS EMOTIONALLY AT-TACHED AND INTELLECTUALLY REMOVED AS POSSI-BLE....

> *ALL LOVE,*
>
> *m*
>
> *PS REMEMBER: THE LEADING CAUSE OF DEATH IS BIRTH....*

Wowza. Gives me a new take on GF. While I feel like a sneaky bastard, it blows my mind how much old people have already done that nobody would guess from seeing them. They haven't always looked like bloated spiders.

Unable to stop my snooping, I yank open another drawer. This one's heaped with papers. I pull out a stack. Some are college essays. There's one on Shakespeare's *Winter's Tale* (B+, "*beware of purple prose!* "); another comparing *Walden* with *Walden Two* (A-, "*some excellent points!* "). Then there's something longer—it's stapled and clipped in two groups. The typewriter here looks funny, the ink's slightly smeared. I've seen this kind of thing before. It's called a carbon—the way they made copies in pre-Xerox days. There's a title: *Blind Angel.* Below, there's a name: *by Jonathan Wainwright, III.* Under that, in green ink: *For Henry, mi amigo, mon semblable, my room-mate, mon frere*

December 12, 1971

Damn. I weigh the sheaf in my hand. Word count alone is impressive. Takes me weeks to eek a graph. Dad was serious way young. I drop to the floor and proceed to inhale it like crack.

PROLOGUE: ART AND MAGIC

A man in a tuxedo stands alongside a baby elephant on the brightly lit stage of a dinner theatre in Las Vegas. He smiles at the audience of bored and tipsy diners. Lost in a world not of her making, the elephant gazes pensively into the middle distance. The man then turns to the elephant, leans over and, with a heave, tosses her into the stunned crowd. Screams shake the room until...people realize the elephant hurtling at them like a canon ball has disappeared. Long silence while they take this in. It's like...magic! Our modest Merlin coughs into his sleeve. "Ladies and gentlemen...." For the next ten minutes, he proceeds to unpack his own trick. He rubs it in: mirrors, of course, plus a projector and a few other special effects. By the time he's done, every last vestige of enchantment and mystery have disappeared, along with the elephant. Every trick we do is like this, he says.

By robbing magic of its, well, magic, he's pissed a lot of people off. After all, the audience already knew the trick was a trick. They're not fools, though they paid top dollar to be fooled. Why rob them of the childish wish embedded inside every magic act: that the invisible forces at the heart of the universe are accessible to a handful of initiates, most of whom are on our side? Why snuff hope's brief candle? Why not fan the flames instead?

But the performer is, at heart, an artist, and like all that ilk, he's got the missionary urge. He's fired by a belief there are at least a few folks out there who'd rather know how the machinery works than live in ignorance. It is to them he speaks.

Still, why cut through what one philosopher called the necessary illusions on which we feed? Isn't that cruel? But the artist isn't trying to spoil our fun. On the contrary, he's aiming to enhance it—to push it to a level few in his audience knew possible. It's been that way ever since fiction's granddaddy, Miguel de Cervantes, launched the jaunty La Manchan on a jaded world. Winking Cervantes never asked us to suspend our belief. Rather he invited us to believe differently—to listen with the wisdom of the child to his tale for adults. Disillusionment has always been the artist's reason for being: it made her who she is as surely as water whelped the whale and the cocoon exhaled a butterfly.

In an age such as ours, the importance and value of disillusionment can't be overestimated. We live in a culture whose economy runs on the sale of fantasies. Its success in blurring the boundary between spectacle and art has contributed mightily to our national stupefaction. Art isn't to be enjoyed as a respite from "real life." Art intends *to be* some thing. Art worthy of the name is life ablaze at full intensity. Not a transit space, but a place of arrival. Work that aspires to art gives us what we need yet can't name until we meet it, like an unexpected lover. It bewilders us the way spring always does after an infernal winter.

The goal of the imperial illusionist is to persuade us to fear each other, to compete with each other, to strive against each other. The writer who matters recognizes this and is not deceived. He is a free man, a free woman, who knows what to damn, and what to praise.

We read for power. And power comes from seeing things as they are, even when that's not to our liking. Like the scientist, the novelist, the poet, the memoirist push past appearances toward essences and deep structures. How else can we begin to understand who we ourselves are, and why we're here? Disillusionment may well be a prerequisite for love. Until then, we have romance, which is what the earliest novels were called. They gave their audiences caricatures in place of characters. The representation of ideal and the real sides of human personality hadn't been integrated and the effect was to feed our fantasies without stimulating our imagination.

As a girl, my mother tried to stay abreast of contemporary European fiction and poetry. She kept lists, a reading diary. Some days she registers four novels completed. From her I first heard the names of Selma Lagerloff, Adam Mickewiecz, Grazia Deledda, Par Lagerkvist, and even Marquez, whom she read in Ukrainian translation before I got it in English. I suspect a few of the names might be unfamiliar to readers, yet in their day....Selma Lagerloff was the first woman to win the Nobel Prize in Literature; Grazia Deledda, from the isolated island of Sardinia, was the second. I've no doubt my mother's reading strengthened her, enlarging her sense of who she was and what was possible. It enabled her to weather the war and a refugee's life soul intact by keeping open another dimension deep in herself which couldn't be hurt by the turbulent world outside her.

We read for power, remembering that nothing matches the weight of all we don't know and never will. Not directly. Our unconscious is the giant serpent whose spine we glimpse rippling just below earth's crust as it lightly brushes air. There's only one way to tap—to "know"—the unknowable. I mean the path of dreams, whose twists and turns are familiar only to a handful of sublimely patient souls. But that's where all the real action is.

4

After reading for almost an hour, I put the manuscript down and walk to the window. The story following the prologue is about the poet Arthur Rimbaud, who apparently took part in all kinds of crazy political shit while writing poems no one could understand which were mainly about his fucking this other poet named Verlaine. If they did this kind of shit in the nineteenth century, before the Internet, how are we surprised by where we are today?

I don't know what makes me dizzier—what I've just read, or what I'm looking at: the ziggy world out there, or the even stranger one inside my skull? Among other things, I realize I know like nothing about Dad's mom, who died long before I was born. He never talked about her.

I won't pretend I understood everything I just read any better than I do that bastard Rilke, but I see the drift: *get out of here, out of your room, your cell, your sty,* it says, *and live! Don't be afraid!* There's song and glory to be had out there.

In the buildings that surround the park are millions, crawling over each other—only, they're not like ants at all. As nature specials tell us, ants work together. In the Amazon, millions of them lock like spindly Lego in a living hive. People just won't do that. They'd rather nibble at each other, tear off bits and pieces here and there until there's nothing left. Makes you think we're not all of one tribe.

* * *

"Repeat," I hear the therapist shout (why? Far as I know GF's hearing is fine): "Apples elephants igloos orangutans *und.*" I try it myself, tripping up on *orangutans* und. Orangutans *und.* But I'm feeling restless, and weirdly hungry. After my age-long internment in the apartment, stoked by a toke, I'm ready to take on the world. "There a good diner in the neighborhood?" I ask.

The therapist turns to GF, who enunciates like a star pupil: "Sarno's. Three blocks down. Need money?"

"Thanks, GF. Madeline has provided," I assure him.

His intelligence turns out to be good: three blocks away, I find Sarno's. My waitress is blond and tall and plump, a dead-ringer for every zaftig blond you've ever seen. I think they mass produce them somewhere. Thank God. The way she takes my order, I suspect she likes me. When I tell her I want a chocolate shake, she nods like I'm a genius. Don't have to be one to think like one, I always say. I scan for a name tag but get snagged on what looks like a nipple peeking out from a black bra. Before the eggs even arrive, the air crackles like bacon. (I decide to break my pattern because eggs cost more, and I want to impress her). She tells me to enjoy, and I plan to. I look around at the other waitresses. None are half as hot as her, and I don't see them giving their people the kinds of smiles and looks I'm getting. By the time the home-fries are history, I think it may be love. The hell with Dad, Rene, the past. I'm moving on. Already older than Rimbaud—it's getting late! My eyes follow her like secret service agents guarding the president.

I'm pretty sure she's into it too. She leans close to ask if I want anything else.

"Heather," I say, finding her tag. She jumps like it's a secret. "Hea-*ther*," I repeat, slowly. "Great name."

Her vague blue eyes fix on mine. "Here's the check." The way she says it leaves room for interpretation.

A text tickles my thigh. Word from Klyt: *Didn't you tell me Gina was a lesbian?* Me: *I said she was Lebanese.*

Klyt reminds me of Astro. We should never have done what we did. I swear it had nothing to do with his being black. Call it the Fog of War. Faulty intelligence. Idiocy. Even as I say it, I wonder: Was it really out of nowhere? I know his life's a lot different from mine because he's black. We've talked about it lots of times yet talking only gets you so far. And now the President is black, it's even more confusing. But could it be we thought it easier to do it to Astro because of that?

A minute later I spot Heather flirting with a fat man in a suit a few tables over. *Me blud goz kold.* She must sense it because immediately afterward she reappears and asks if I want anything else. Him to die, I don't have the balls to say. Air ices between us. Downed again by my own cowardice. This happens every time I think I feel something between me and whoever, and just as I'm about to make a move, it all goes up in smoke.

Another text, this from Rene: *Worried a/Astro. Call me.* Not good. Can people feel each other's thoughts?

Meanwhile, Heather has moved on to bantering with a young couple at the next table. Her back is to me but I hear her laughing. Maybe threesomes? People bore so easily. She stands there forever, then comes by and picks up Mom's credit card. She returns with the receipt, mumbles thank you without looking. Women. Oh man. I need to do something to put her out of my mind. The fat man rises. I decide to follow him. Before going, I leave a tip so big Heather will probably orgasm.

Outside, I put on my mirrored sunglasses. He huffs up CPW four blocks to 66th, then turns down to the zoo. Five years ago, the Keepers dragged us here to see the Christo Gates. Asia insisted she wanted to go to the zoo. I hated zoos ever since we visited Franklin Park in Dorchester. The lion there looked even more depressed than Mom. It lay on the ground, staring at the sky, blinking and yawning. "Eat a human," I whispered. "Feel free to start with Dad." (Just kidding, big D). Anyway, we managed to get lost and I had to use the cell phone Dad gave me for emergencies. By this time, Asia was screaming so loud I worried they might toss *her* in a cage.

I'm standing on a little hill in bright sun somewhere in the middle of the park. The world's gone green again. A rabbit snuffles on the curled green edge of things, when who do I see hurrying up the path but that wiley Brazilian, Serafina. She's wearing a red kerchief and sunglasses like a Kardashian, head down, limping, hobbled by a broken heel. What's she up to? Was she Henry's mistress before becoming his nurse? Maybe I should see where she's going.

I follow her through the park. When she emerges on Fifth Avenue, she looks over her shoulder like she senses something. I stop and let a group of French tourists wash over me. A girl waves a whirligig around like a wand until a little boy snatches it out of her hand and runs off. "*Alors, alors!*" the mother cries, but the boy ignores her.

I step out of the swarm to see her booking it up 66th. Where's she going, this wild side of things? I pass portrait artists, chachka vendors, pretzel sellers, stalled cars and cabs, and cross just as she turns the corner on Madison. The mansions don't impress me. They're gray, like they're wearing suits with too much starch, and bow-ties. Not quite the Paris Commune here. At least the neighborhood's got lots of dogs, I'll give it that. A labradoodle leaking on a tire's the kind of sight I like to see.

At Second Avenue, Serafina makes a left, a right, moving quickly, arms rowing, like she's late. I stay half a block behind. The red scarf makes her hard to miss. Finally, she pauses in front of a church. For the neighborhood, it's modest. I read the sign: St. Catherine of Sienna. Instead of going up the front stairs, she heads down an alley, toward a door in the back, and goes in.

Is she having an affair with a priest? Mom used to go to the Unitarian Church in Harvard Square for political meetings. Sometimes I think none of what Mom did was crazy. Maybe she couldn't fix the world, but at least she tried. It was only when she stopped that she began going nuts.

I suppose I could always just ask Serafina what's up. The direct approach, as uncommon as common sense itself.

On my way back, I see an old lady pushing a baby carriage—clearly a grandmother, helping out her kids—and, naturally, I think of our own maybe-kid-in-progress. Would Mom do that for me—help out with the maybe-kid? Would Dad?

Halfway into the park, there's a lake. I clamber up a boulder and look out at the people rowing boats across the water: entire families pulling together, singing and laughing and looking so happy, it's driving me crazy. All we want is some place to feel safe, and home just ain't it. I sit down on the rock and close my eyes.

* * *

Thinking back over these last weeks, I realize I too have been a little insane. Let me tell you why Klyt and I were suspended.

First: We're having an assembly to discuss career options. Everyone, including freshmen, is herded into the state of-the-art auditorium. The presentation's by the career counselor, a nice older woman who used to work as a nurse's aide at Youville, a hospital down the street. She's always been kind to me and I don't have a bad word to say about her. This isn't about her, though. The point is I hacked into her computer and replaced a few of the web-sites she planned to take us to with some of my personal favorites. So after reminding us how important study and college are, she begins talking about what those who won't be going might do with their lives. Her PowerPoint presentation includes a list of possible alternative professions, from auto mechanic to software technician to hospital orderly. To give us a fuller idea of what these might involve, she clicks onto a website containing a brief film about "alternative jobs" for "when college just won't fit." Never mind the reasons why—because parents would need to sell a few organs or female children to pay for it. She clicks, and there it is, my handiwork: a free site about....fisting. Suddenly the giant screen fills with the image of a blond hunk stuffing his fist up the ass of a guy with a shaved head. It lasts about two seconds before the scream and the crash of the computer announce the end of the assembly.

That was part one. And probably nobody would have bothered tracking down who had set that up if there hadn't been a Part Two.

We chose Astro to experiment on. For one thing, he's the smallest. He'd be the easiest to hold down, Klyt insisted. We didn't even think about his brother. Or that, as Rene reminded us later, his father is Nation of Islam. Didn't cross our minds. We got this idea into our heads because we're both fans of *24*, the TV show with Kiefer Sutherland going after terrorists. I mean, it's awful, but these things make you think. Who ever thought about waterboarding, until our ex-veep made it his sport? Mom and Dad talked about it. Our teachers. Our friends. We thought it would be funny—not like it was torture. We decided to do it in school because it has an excellent nursing staff and if anything went wrong, the hospital's a block away. We chose a friend because we were pretty sure he wouldn't report us. We hoped that later he'd think it was funny too.

We rendezvoused in the Boy's Room, like we often did after lunch. Klyt and I came in together. Astro was already there, combing his hair in front of the mirror. All we were going to do was hold his head under the sink. Nothing more, nothing harsher—bad enough, I know. We didn't get close. First Klyt said to him "So, you think waterboarding isn't like torture?" This was Astro's firm position. "No, man," he said. "Just a dunkin', dude." Next thing you know Klyt's got him in a head-lock. He's laughing. So is Astro. And so am I as I grab his legs and lift him up. He kicks me away and I release him. Maybe we were a little high. It got crazy. He said stop. We laughed harder. We didn't stop. Klyt had his arms and I had his legs again and he was shouting pretty loud then but Klyt was laughing so hard, we didn't hear the principal walk in. Wouldn't surprise me if they've got web cams in the johns. It was a moment, I'll tell you. Dumb beyond belief. Our own small evil.

We are more penitent than Judas. I only hope we don't have to hang ourselves to prove it. We didn't think what we wanted to do was violent. Really. We didn't think Astro would be mad—for long, anyway. Or that it might scare him—or piss him off, or hurt him. We thought he'd think it was funny. He's the one who said it wasn't torture. But, when I think about it, I'm pretty sure I wouldn't want someone to do that to me.

* * *

Two weeks before this happened, Klyt, Astro, Rene and I were sitting in the clubhouse after rehearsal, choking on a mushroom and artichoke pizza Rene ordered and which was more than a little gross. The place has a skylight my parents installed years ago. This spring we've had to push a bucket underneath to catch the rainwater.

We were practicing to be famous. Because that means going on a lot of talk shows, we wanted to be ready to address whatever comes up: global warning, Sudan, Wikileaks (go Julian!), Haiti, mayo chiki, and Lady Gaga. We were discussing something our Biology teacher said in class that day, just twenty-four hours before my little attempt to brighten the American educational experience. Mrs. Tardy was explaining the latest breakthrough in neurology. While she spoke, my eyes roved from Klyt's knobby knees to Rene, who was wearing one of her mother's old peasant blouses. The embroidered flaps on the plunging neckline lay loose around her small, tight breasts.

Seems they've isolated the place in the brain where we make moral judgments. They claim they can change our views with a magnet. It's more complicated than that, but that's the drift. One of Dad's a-hole Big-H colleagues immediately began saying how this proves we don't have a soul, since if we did, they couldn't change our minds with just a magnet.

Didn't take Rene long to riddle that with holes. Her dark eyes fixed on us. "Just because it takes time to develop a capacity for moral judgment, like building muscles, doesn't make those judgments questionable," said Rene. "That you can destroy that capacity with a magnet doesn't negate what *was* there. So moral observations are rooted in the body. So what? It only proves they're like muscles which gotta be used, or they go soft. Use it or lose it. And it has nothing to do with the soul, which may well be amoral anyway."

Her hand slashed the air in a crippling chop. Man down, and out. No doubt.

We stared with open mouths. She wears no make-up. Her long eyes and short hair black as my old MacBook. Talking to her is like bungee-jumping down the Grand Canyon.

"This is why the Chinese will rule the world," Klyt said after a moment's silence.

Rene says she might do a double major in nuclear physics and archaeology at the University of Chicago. Whenever she starts prattling about string theory, I get a pocket rocket. It's sick, but that's me. I sing and celebrate myself. You do the same.

This was also the day after Rene told me she might be pregnant. Only a few weeks ago, but it feels like a century. That night, I couldn't sleep. Being a dad isn't exactly something I wanted. Not yet—and maybe not ever. The alternative's not pretty, though. And once it's gone, it's gone. No going back. I think of Astro's brother, who once slapped me in the back of the head for no good reason while we were playing *Drone* on the Xbox. How many times Astro said he wished his brother Macro dead. And now he is.

BEY-AH!

BEY-AH!

I'm about to cross the street outside the Park when I notice a black and yellow espresso cup clattering along the sidewalk toward the curb. A turtle, at the edge of the road. I leap forward, scoop it up. It yanks its rubbery green and yellow-speckled neck into its shell. Anywhere but here, I'd think it strange, but we've all seen the clips of alligators in sewers and pythons slithering down Broadway. I hold the turtle close. The shell is cold and hard between my fingers.

Outside the building, I stop to chat with Ivan, the doorman, who asks about the turtle. Bends for a look, but it's shy. Then I ask him where he got his accent.

"Moskva."

Would *I* like being a doorman? The none-too-shabby royal blue uniform, epaulets, gold buttons. "But you have *hardly* any accent," I backpedal. Flattery's a Molly to adults.

He then garbles a tale from which I gather he was just a boy when someone, man or rhomboid I don't catch, strode into the house he shared with hornets, and raped the squid in a basket of urchins and a juniper bush, until the blue eye burst, which made the mad dogs go away. Something like that.

The way he looks at me, I bet he's thinking how great it would be to be fifteen again. Man, would I like to remind him: fifteen is the biggest suck-hole of an age ever invented. Shitload worse than fourteen, which itself already made thirteen look good. And don't get me started on twelve! I mean, you're mostly clueless about everything—school, love, food, or what it means to be a sane human being, since you've never met the type. I'd have high hopes for sixteen, if my life weren't such a mess.

A plump babe with a box from Bloomie's hustles in. She grins at Ivan, who looks down and holds the door. She glances over her shoulder and rolls on.

"Mrs. Duncan, 11C," he sighs and lowers his head.

"You watch out there, Ivan," I say, giving him the "primo" hand sign—another treasure from the Triads—while Davis wiggles his legs.

* * *

Henry sits in his place before the picture window, looking out at streets down which he'll never walk again. While staring at his back, I hear what sounds like sobbing from the kitchen, and I freeze.

As if on cue, Rene texts: *Call.*

"Welcome back, Jonathan," says the GF.

Suddenly I want to race straight through the glass, go soaring across the sky above the city where, for a moment, I might see, and for once understand, what it is I'm seeing.

Sometimes I open Photo Booth on the iPad and just stare at my face. Not because I want to see *it*. I'm trying to see my thoughts. The craziest ideas run through my head, yet when I look at myself, I'm exactly the same as when all is quiet in my sicko brain. Was it like this for Rimbaud? Did he really see the alphabet in color and smell sounds? What if what I want to do with my life is drive a taxi? Or become a porn star? Or a serial killer? Sometimes I wish there was a guy doling out IDs that tell you who you'll be forever. There's always this voice, a feeling, racing inside me, and I wish I knew who it was. Just now it said: *Zumbafockwadowsky!* Faces should show everything, like those screen visualizers on iTunes, morphing with each note.

"Hey, GF," I finally reply. As I set my pack and, without thinking, Davis, on the couch, I hear the sobs again.

* * *

I feel her before seeing her—the way the air changes when a storm's about to land: that extra stillness in the anxious lull, a held breath, then a door slams and I whirl around, expecting Serafina.

Instead, a girl skinny as a supermodel rushes in, wiping her cheeks with her knuckles. Gold bangles jangle up and down her slight, bronze arms. She's wearing a cut-off denim jacket, a post-it-sized black skirt, and more rings on her fingers than Saturn. Sunglasses crown her big orange hair. Stiletto heels like knitting needles. Seeing me, she does a double-take.

"Ola," she whispers sullenly, obviously annoyed by my presence. "Who are you?"

"No," I counter: "Who are *you?*" In my god-father's apartment with no one around.

Some faces hit you like the Hot Coffee mod of Grand Theft Auto; others come encrypted with glasses, or a bad haircut, or a sleepless night. This one was coded by experts. If faces are music, she is Nirvana. And, something stranger, like we'd met before—say in Egypt, after dying, in a Pharaoh's tomb. Wild pomegranate hair and Cleopatra eyes.

"Meu nome e Beyah." Did GF order an escort? If so, does he know she's underage?

"What are you doing here?" I ask.

"I asked you first," she holds her ground.

"I live here," I say casually.

"Really? Since when? Serafina's my mom," she says, tilting her head to the left, eyes flashing.

I thought Serafina said her family's in Brazil.

"Beyah," she repeats, in case I'm slow.

"Bey-ah. Yes, you said. Nice to meet you." I watch her long fingers twist a lock of frizzy hair.

"Deleitado encontra-lo," she rasps. "And you are?" Everything sounds better in Portuguese. Beneath that denim vest, I swear the girl's swathed in dental floss.

"You up from Brazil?" I'm confused. Did I miss something again? "I'm Jonathan. He's my godfather." I gesture toward Henry, who says, "Turn me around, please, Jonathan."

Her eyes widen, flatlining to slits while her fingers pirouette around the fringes of her stringy top.

I walk up to his wheelchair, thinking: first I see Serafina in the Park and now her kid's here. What's the scam? They grifters? I've seen the movies. Chick looks like she knows her way around. "Here you go," I say, putting him face to face with our visitor.

"Believe it or not, this really is my godson." he says, addressing her.

She smiles, waving the cigarette. "You don't mind, sir, do you?"

Their familiarity confounds my confidence.

"Never have," he nods.

She and Mom must be the last women smokers on the planet.

"Is that what my mother told you?"

"What?"

"That we're in Brazil?"

I weigh the implications of telling the truth against my natural instinct to lie. "In a *favela*," I say.

"Jeezus, Mary, and Joseph!" She rolls her eyes and her mouth drops in a theatrical gasp. A gust of shimmer ripples. Or maybe it's her bangles. "Doesn't make my job any easier, does she?"

"What's your job? Why were you crying?"

"I'm not crying."

"You were."

She turns her head this way and that like she's expecting a visitor. "Anyway, I gotta go." But makes no move.

"What happened?"

"Long story," she shrugs. And where *is* Serafina? Something's not adding up. "Got checks for her to sign." Her eyes range nervously around the room.

"So where *do* you live?" I ask.

She tips her ash, leans back against a chair, hand on hip, hisses: "Jersey." Which, on her lips, sounds exotic as Madagascar. "Like who can afford New York, right?" As her eyes stray, I wonder if she recognizes the Warhol behind the sofa. The pianos, the other instruments. But she's been here before. "How about you?" she asks.

"Boston," I say.

"That like Harvard?"

I shrug apologetically (I'm almost as bad as Dad). The brand has more legs than the human centipede. Suddenly she yelps. (A yelper, like mom!) I look down. Davis has fallen to the floor and is inching along the carpet. His neck rotates slowly.

"Who that?"

"Davis." I say, squatting. As though hearing his name, Davis stops dead. Beyah grinds out her smoke and kneels beside me. I smell eucalyptus. She brings her lips right near his green and yellow head:

"Mr. Davis, how do you do?" Davis retracts into his shell. "Where'd you get him? Where you gonna put him? Turtles are a lot of work."

"Don't know yet." We're eye level, so close I feel her breath on my lips. Her skin stretches before me like a beach.

"Don't know yet? You bring this beautiful wild thing into your house without a place to put him, and no plans? What kind of a person are you?" She looks like she might slap me.

Her anger throws me off. "I just found him, on the street!"

"He's not a toy, you know." Calming down. "Something from the kitchen maybe," she suggests, pushing up from the floor.

I palm Davis, who digs so deep into himself he'll soon be seeing God, and follow her.

"You're stressing him out. He thinks he's soup."

After a few minutes of foraging, rejecting mixing bowls and salad spinners, during which Davis doesn't peek out once, I'm about ready to give up when Beyah cries, *Eu sai*! She yanks the vegetable bin out of the fridge, dumping the lettuce scraps and a few battered tomatoes onto the counter.

"What'll we do with the veggies?"

"Mom will figure it out," she shrugs. She fills the bin with an inch of water, grabs a couple of little dishes and lays them down. Rocks! After I resettle Davis in his new home, I carry him into the living room for the GF to admire. "Look, Senhor Henry! You have a visitor," Beyah says.

"Fine-looking creature," he says.

"What do turtles eat," I wonder.

"Lots of things. Got any crickets?"

"How could you possibly know?" I stare at this half-nude walking Wikipedia.

"Three brothers and a sister," she replies. "Rabbits, gerbils, an iguana, a tarantula, two dogs, a turtle. They've had everything. Their crazy uncles brought them. Only the tarantula and dogs made it. I hate pets. They can eat veggies," she says impatiently.

We return to the kitchen and attack the produce spilled across the counter. She slices carrots like she knows a knife.

"Too much?" I ask. She ignores me, grabs two fistfuls, and I follow her back to the living room.

"Turtles know what's enough," she snaps, distributing the food around the terrarium.

"Is Beyah like a common name in Brazil?"

She pauses, brings a carrot to her lips. "It's Beatriz, *stupido*," she explains.

"So your Dad and you stay home while your mom works here?" I fish, though what for I can't say.

"I gotta get back," she says, avoiding my question, scattering a fistful of broccoli around the pond. "Going up to the Portuguese Pines for the Memorial Day weekend," she adds.

"And your dad?"

"Enough with the inquisition, dude."

Even as we banter, something moves between us: our words coil like wires around a magnet which turns, ringing us in a protective current. I can almost see the braid of light shimmying around and through her, and encircling me.

I feel myself unmooring, drifting ever further from familiar shores. The way she stands, arms braced defensively, reminds me of those girls who scared me in the halls of seventh grade. I dreamed about them in the dead of night: tough, hot and wild like the wind, their secret bruised hearts buried, open only to tattooed night-stalkers and aspiring prison guards. This time, I'm not scared. The opposite. There's heart in her delivery and oh man, oh her eyes.

She returns to the kitchen for a towel with which she wipes the glass coffee table around the terrarium. GF follows every move.

"How old are you?" I ask, on safer ground.

She just stares at me.

Another text from Rene, this time: *!Call!*

Towel in hand, she turns to me. We're like an old couple cleaning up after a party. Another lock of hair loses its struggle to stay up, a tendril loops her ear. Her face isn't carved or chiseled: it's the original from which the others spawned. Is there anything in the world more mysterious than a girl? Calculus is processed cheese beside one of these.

"You hungry?" I ask. "There's this great diner down the block." (That would show the waitress!)

She folds the towel. "Thanks, but I gotta get back." She picks up a fake leopard-skin bag big enough to hold a leopard.

Stop, heart. You can't leave. I've only just found you. Stick around a few centuries. What I say is: "When you coming back?"

"I'm in Brazil, remember? Don't tell my mother you saw me."

"What about the checks? Want me to give them to her?"

"That's okay. I'll forge her signature," she sighs. "Been done before." Reaches into her bag for another smoke.

"Didn't hear that," GF says.

"Wait!" I shout.

She turns. "What you staring at?"

I'm frozen. Something heavy's going on inside. How deep? The body's a relatively small place. You get that pretty clearly in Manhattan. A potted plant inside a jungle. Despite several growth spurts, I remain this side of five feet six. My chest must be less than one square foot of real estate, yet somehow I feel

I'm carrying a planet inside me. I want badly, and from nowhere, to spend more time with her, although I think that's not
so smart. This may have to do with Rene cramping my style.
Maybe. Granted, fatherhood's a job. But does it mean I have to
give up all the other girls on the planet, forever? Isn't that a little nuts?

She's halfway gone and I'm desperate. Is this normal? Her
heels tick the floor like a time bomb.

"Wait!" I shout again.

"What?" She whirls around, this time sounding pissed.

"I'm writing a book."

"Really?" Her skepticism kills me, but she stops. She drops
her bag off her shoulder, holds it before her with both hands,
head to the side, like *show me.*

"And you're going to be in it!"

"I am? Who will I be?" Unexpectedly struck chord. Frankly, I'm astonished she believes me. I hardly believe myself.

"Yourself. Beyah. Just as you are. In a book you get to be
more yourself than you ever can in life." Just as you are, is all I
ask of this owl-eyed, half-nude razor of a girl who's ribboned
me to pieces on the floor. Such thoughts I have.

"Cool. But listen, in the book, can I wear contacts? I hate
my glasses," she says.

"You're not wearing any."

"I know. I can't really see what you look like. But you seem
nice." She makes a face. Then pulls down her sunglasses.

"It's not a movie. Nobody will see your glasses. Which you
don't wear anyway."

"Good luck."

"Oh, look, he's eating." I point to Davis, my voice rising. She steps forward, hunches down. As we bend over the bin, a lace of hair brushes my wrist and it's like someone tossed a toaster into a bathtub.

Davis munches on a carrot.

"Don't you have school?" I ask, taking advantage of a fresh opening.

"Dropped out," she shrugs, swinging her bag.

"So did I," I lie.

"I gotta go. Once the brats start acting up, it's game over. So, *bom-por, meu amor!*"

"Your English is really good," I say, forgetting she was born here.

"See ya."

Sound the chords of *London Calling*. Rene. Shit. "Excuse me." I grab the phone. "I have to talk to you," Rene says. "Can I call you back?" I say, hanging up without waiting for her answer. The minute I do, I remember what day it is. As Beyah walks toward the elevator, a voice inside me shouts: speak, speak! "Got a number, I mean for emergencies?"

She looks over her shoulder: "Sorry, kid."

The elevator door slides shut. I fall to the couch and stare at GF. Does he know? Can he feel it? Did he see? He nods: "They forget," he says cryptically. Of course I know what he means. The crazy power they have.

I get up. I pace. Pick up the ashtray, run my fingers down the bin's rim, crouch to the floor where she just stood, wander through the kitchen, studying the veggies on the counter. I'm like Garbo as I memorize the room. What happened here will help make history.

* * *

Then: panic! If I don't do something, she'll fade away, like that grinning cat. Not even her smile will remain. What's my next step? How can I get this right?

I remember how intense it was reading "m"'s letters to the GF—and that's it. A letter. I'll write Beyah a letter—bet she's never gotten one before. It will be the greatest letter ever written. The last great letter. I shut my eyes, start composing in my head. I don't get far, so I open a doc on the iPad, but that feels cold. The GF's watching. I shrug—you got something better? If anyone understands, it's him. Finally, I pull a pen and pad from my bag and, after a few minutes of nothing, write: *Dear Daylight,*

What next? I've never handwritten a real letter in my life, never mind a love letter. Only one I know who writes, and gets paper letters, is Dad, and, obviously, the GF. From my generation, like zero. Email's feeble, texting's bull. I don't even have her address, but I gotta do something.

"Read me some more," says the GF. He's trying to get my mind off Beyah.

I should tell him the whole story about Rene, and Dad. I'm sure he'd have advice. Thing is, once you ask an adult anything, you sort of feel obliged to do what they say, which doesn't always work. Instead, I read from my latest entry:

Grazia Madesani, nee Deledda, Novelist and Poet, 1871-1936

Her full name was Grazia Maria Cosima Damiana Deledda. Born in Nuoro, on the isle of Sardinia, where her father was a well-off landowner, she had no literary connections, knew nothing about publishing. One day, she picked up a fashion magazine, copied out an address, submitted a story. They ran it. Neighbors called her mother irresponsible for raising a child who wrote love stories.

Emboldened, Grazia sat down and wrote a novel. She sent it to an editor in Rome. To her amazement, he published it. Moreover, "it did quite well." The "racket," as Dad calls it, used to be a lot easier, it seems. Grazia, bless her, stuck with it. Even nabbed a Nobel Prize—but not right away. At first, stores wouldn't carry her books. Every writer, I'm discovering, faces trials.

Grazia's native Sardinia has its own language—and the villages their own dialects. Her mother tongue was called *logudorese sardo.* She was born on the first anniversary of the unification of Italy. In school, she was made to study a foreign language, Italian. Wisely, she too quit—after grade school. School mostly fucks with the mind. Of course, in her case, it's because she was a girl. Her maternal grandfather lived like a hermit and talked to his animals. Grazia said the best present she ever got was a *mouflon*, a copper-colored, short-haired, wild native sheep. But life in Sardinia was hard. Bandits flourished and the elements ruled. In winter, many people froze to death. Food was also scarce and, one dark day, her beloved mouflon became dinner.

As a newly converted semi-vegetarian, I've got to register my shock. All carnivores are cannibals, but there's a special circle in hell for people who eat their pets. The obstacles this presents when writing about basically heroic figures like Grazia are greater than you imagine. I have to say, though, some of what I'm learning gives me new respect for writers, a thing I didn't think possible after a lifetime of Dad.

A common motif in Grazia's work is the corruption of priests forced by Rome to stifle their instincts, which rear up and bite them no matter how long they pray or scourge themselves. It's all over the news. Long as I can remember I've been hearing about it. Priests should be forced to marry—boys, if they like. Then they'd get it. What the rest of us are dealing with.

* * *

A few minutes later, Serafina comes in. She's sweaty and distracted. I'm no Sherlock but she has a run in her stocking, and that broken heel. Henry raises his head.

"What you reading?" she asks, smiling.

I sit up straighter. She is the Mother of Beyah. Which changes everything. "My book."

"You writin' a book, *amor*?" Her eyes widen, head rolls back. She's clearly impressed. "What's it about?"

"Like I said before: The importance of literature in the age of Twitter," I confide. At that moment, another text from Rene: *CALL ME!* I hate it when people use all caps.

"Boy, you even smarter than I thought, Mr. Einstein." Not a trace of irony in her voice. "Good for you," she adds. "I love poetry. You know Fernando Pessoa?"

"Of course I know Fernando," I say. (I have never heard of Fernando, but give me a few minutes on Wikipedia and I'll write you a book). "My Dad teaches at Harvard." The H-bomb scores again. In the bonus round, I make my move: "Something I meant to tell Beyah..."

"You met Beyah?" She takes a step back, blinking disbelief, as if I said I'd just blown a bone with the Pope.

"She was here when I came in," I blurt, forgetting my vow.

"That girl!" Her expression changes to a scowl. "I tell her not to come. Should have stayed in school. I tell her."

"I thought you said she was in Brazil. In a *favela*."

She looks over at Henry, who is listening intently: "Jonatan, this is a story I can't tell right now. It's bad she bothered you with our troubles." Her face gets this dark, worried look.

Not my aim to rat Beyah out—but I want to know what

these two are hiding.

"She's a brilliant girl," I assure Serafina. "I was delighted to meet her. We were discussing a book."

"Beyah was reading a book?"

"She's an astonishingly well-read girl," I said.

Serafina shakes her head: "A mother is always the last to know!" Her moods shift so fast, I better land this before the weather changes.

"I was wondering if I might have her number. I've got a few more recommendations." At which point GF snorts. I shoot him a look. This time it's Serafina who does the chin-to-chest.

"Sure, honey, sure."

I rise and hand her the notebook and pen. "Just put it right there."

"These are all your words, eh?" She admires my scrawl.

"Thank you very much," I say, looking over what she's written. "That's 908?"

"Yes, honey, New Jersey."

"Cool. Again, sincerest thanks. Maybe I should also get her address so I can mail that reading list we talked about."

"Reading list!"

"If you don't mind," I say, handing back the pad. "Now, don't let me interrupt you. I'm sure you've work to do. Oh, one last thing."

She's growing suspicious—but of what?

"Portuguese Pines."

"Yes?"

"What is that?"

"She told you about that? My my. It's a place my brothers bought years ago. Upstate New York, where some of the community goes in the summers."

"If I could get that too…"

She raises an eyebrow. "Sure, *querido*, sure." Serafina writes down the address and, after one last quizzical look, sweeps off to the kitchen while I turn to Henry. I feel his brain working….when a ping summons me to my email. Rene, forwarding the video of the year as selected by the *New Scientist*, a British web-site she's always reading. And what do you think it is? Pure coolity, like a python swallowing a Hummer? Dream on. No, my friends, it's the first ever footage of ovulation, filmed by an endoscope shoved up the Big V. I watch the ovary at the tip of the fallopian tube, tiny feelers like you see on the lip of a Venus fly trap, or spider legs closing on a fly. Is she trying to sell me or just gross me out? Runner up, incidentally, is self-folding paper useful in origami…Something for Mom.

But it gets me thinking. A child: cells multiplying, as if life itself was a kind of cancer. After she leaves, I continue reading to the GF, but my mind's all over the place—with Mom, Dad, Beyah, Rene, the future, and the past.

* * *

The pain and madness around her deepened Grazia. Her subjects became destiny, will, and human suffering: "*Forze occulte, fatali, spingono luomo al bene o al male; la natura stessa, che sembra perfetta, e sconvolta dale violenze di una sorte ineluttabile."* Or, to put it another way, occult forces drive us, and nature has in it a darkness all its own. In the meantime, she had to take over the family business, run the olive press, keep accounts.

Life is suffering.

* * *

When the GF falls asleep at last, I decide to go back to my room and finish my letter to Beyah. For inspiration I yank open a drawer, pull out a fistful of letters from "m," and settle down on the floor. This one's in sepia ink no less.

Cherest Henri,
Two letters in one day mon ami that is indeed spoiling me.
Having all this time to myself when i can do nothing constructive i have a good time analyzing our affair. i am very upset with not being able to control any of my emotions toward you, i miss you so desparately and i keep telling myself, "not normal, when do i start handling things maturely" that sort of thinking leads to instant depression as the arguments are infinite. i start to worry about my age (19!), money, children, jesus, i could make myself sick, the problem is i refuse to believe i have any fear of making a 'comitment' whatever that means, it is difficult to grasp what i am trying to say even for me...
And there's Albert—your old roomate's been making eyes at me, you should know that. Now I'm not his student anymore, it's

fair.

Henry I am definitely going crazy—not only that but I read in the newest Psychology Today *how I have all the blossoming tendencies of a schizo.*

Only 26 days till the shore...

Love love,

m

It's only with this third letter that I really take in the initial "m"—so small and elegant, the brown ink like an old photograph. I've seen that "m" before. More than once. In fact, I've seen it often, and quite recently. The ink is different but the shape of the letter is unmistakable: lower case, the slanted strokes small, fragile, determined. The realization comes to me gradually, then all at once, like the flu: the last time I saw that "m" was four days ago. It sat at the bottom of a note about sesame tofu and was probably still pinned by a little square magnet to the old, noisy refrigerator in our kitchen, where Mom (aka Madeline, aka "m") put it to remind Dad and me that she was paying closer attention to the culinary side of our lives than we perhaps realized. The love letters I've been reading—and of which I have like ten thousand more to look at—were written to the GF by none other than Madeline, my Mom. "m."

I lie back down on the bed and stare at the ceiling. Is it possible? All these years. Mom and the GF? One guy in the world I thought I could trust. Who was always straight with me. Is it possible? Sounds like she was with him before Dad.

I pull out more letters, lay them out on the bed. Maybe I'm

wrong about the handwriting. I look yet again.

Just then the door opens and Serafina spikes in: "Jonatan, *querido*. You can feed him, yes? I really need to see my baby clams."

"You're flying to Brazil?" I say. Not that I want to provoke her but what I've just found out about Henry and Mom is shifting continents inside me.

She looks at the letters on the bed, then at me, and sighs knowingly. "You say Beyah just here. She need something. You don't understand, *querido*."

Which is true: I'm in the dark, about everything. Like a moth. Why is Serafina lying? Why won't she tell me what's going on? What was she up to at the church? She's breathing hard, her breasts rise and fall. Christ on that gold cross between them has no chance of napping. She tells me she'll be back to-morrow night. She's left meals in the fridge, and a chicken breast on the stove. I ask her to say hi to Beyah.

"I will, darling," she says.

After she's gone, I put away the letters. I peer into the living room where the GF sits at his post by the window. Romeo on wheels. Mother's lover. For how long? Those times we visited, was he sleeping with her?

* * *

Our subject Grazia's sister died of a miscarriage before she could marry her secret lover. Her brother stole money to pay for his hookers. He fathered an illegitimate child, was imprisoned for stealing. After their father died, he wasted the family fortune. Her other brother was an inventor who once built a hot air balloon he floated over the Sardinian mountains. The natives believed they were enjoying a rare visit from the Holy Ghost. Once more we witness the benefits of a religious education. One day something he was working on exploded and burned him, head to toe. To kill the pain, he too started drinking. He knocked on people's doors after midnight, crying the end was at hand. Personally, I think that's always a safe bet.

* * *

After finishing a 'graph, I get up and pace. I count the number of feet from the bed to the door to the window, as though geometry might save me. My thoughts are all over the place. Maybe Mom *is* schizo and I have her genes. And what if Serafina and her family are illegal? Maybe we'll get raided by Homeland Security or the Immigration Service. Beyah's number. 908. What would I say? Serafina will expose my lies. Tomorrow night, when she returns, I'll have to answer for them. So will she.

I lie down on the floor again. At that moment, Rene texts again: *NOW!*

My lips and fingertips feel cold. "Yo," is my inauspicious beginning.

"I've been calling all afternoon. Where you been? Have you had the ringer off? Don't you know what today is?" She's practically shouting.

"Sorry. Kind of crazy here. Sorry. So?" I don't tell her how freaked out I am.

Long pause. "It's happening," she says at last, her voice soft, apologetic, more question than statement.

I stare out into the dark. I don't know what to say. I knew it already.

"I'm scared," she says.

"What of?"

"Everything."

Though I'm feeling that way myself, I have this gut sense my job's not to let her know it. But I can't put my devil-may-care attitude into words. I stare at the letters.

"Jonathan, you there?"

"Yeah."

"Tell me it's going to be okay."

I've never heard her sound like this. "It's gonna be okay," I say, without much *umph*. (Reality check: my family's falling apart, I've been bounced out of school, Rene is with child, and there's Beyah. Does *okay* really cover it?)

"That all you have to say? Not good enough. I'm asking you again: what are we going to do?"

"What?" I mumble, suddenly sounding like GF.

"Don't you dare hang up on me," her voice is steel. "I've listened to you bitch about your parents for a million hours. We're talking about our lives, Jonathan."

"Rene? You there? Can't hear you," I say, killing the call. All I can think of is how, after a band rehearsal, her neck will smell like rubber burning. I stare at the blue square. Not much good can come of this.

I need air. Up on the balcony, the big picture opens before me again.

At night New York's a hive of eyes, a monster with a zillion electrodes, and I'm inside it. I try lighting a joint but the wind keeps blowing out the zippo. I persevere. The river is wide. What kind of fish live in the Hudson? I know I shouldn't have hung up. Knocks me out she's with a douche like me. I am not worthy. But this baby stuff, it's a *de trop,* as Ms. Petraca used to say. Like you order a burger and they bring you the whole cow. I don't even know how to think about it. These writers I'm writing about think they had problems, but I bet not one had this to deal with at fifteen.

* * *

An hour later, I hear him calling my name. I hurry down the hall.

I switch on the light and suddenly the room's ablaze. Looks like a medieval banquet hall, empty and cold, but smells like a john at a bus station. Only furniture's a dresser crowded with squads of bottles, doubled by the mirror to a pharma army. And a bed the size of a small SUV. On the wall, across from it, hangs what at first glance appears to be a photo of a smooth stone wet with rain but then I see that it's, in fact, a moist and slightly open pussy. What will these artists think of next?

Henry's beached across the purple sheets. Looks at me with wide, imploring eyes, and whispers "Bedpan, bedpan."

Scanning the room, I spot that kidney-shaped aluminum

bowl they use in hospitals under the commode. I hurry it to the bed. Henry watches, wordless. Dawns on me I've got to shove it underneath his ass.

I crawl across the mattress. On my knees, I try lifting him from the side. He groans, I drop him, try again. He screams. A grown man's scream is a terrible thing.

"Legs," he blurts. My best approach is to go under the thighs. Though my hands brush places I won't say, eventually I score. The thing is barely secure when I hear a splat and the odor of shit fills the room. His eyes are closed, mouth clamped tight. I turn away until he sighs and I gather he's done.

Not without trouble, I pull the thing out. He's on his side now and can't roll over until he's been cleaned. I inch off the bed, clutching my bounty. It slops in the pan as I carry it, arm extended far from my face, toward the bathroom. Crossing the threshold, I nearly trip on something, my arm jerks up, a turd soars like a rolled flapjack, flopping back into the pan. Lips pinned, breath held, I flush it down the toilet and return with a roll of paper.

Done, I rush to the bathroom and scrub my hands. His wide eyes follow me. Doesn't say word, but I understand him perfectly. We will never speak of this.

I move backwards to the door without taking my eyes off him, switch off the light, and retreat to my room where I try not to think about anything.

* * *

Grazia lived quietly, in Rome, taking care of her adult sons. She kept a regular schedule. She ate a late breakfast, read for two hours, followed by lunch and a nap, then two or three hours of writing. Average rate of production: four pages a day seven days a week, year in and year out. Result: thirty novels and four hundred short stories. Plus articles, plays, a libretto. This insane productivity troubles me. She also had a pet crow, Checcha, who shat on her guests.

The Nobel Prize changed things. When Grazia returned from Stockholm, Mussolini had just been elected. He asked if there was anything Grazia wanted. She requested the release of a friend imprisoned for anti-fascist activities. She was also pals with Antonio Gramsci, a fellow Sardinian and cofounder of the Italian Communist Party. Eventually, she turned her back on society, which always screws you in the end. Why do people torture themselves over it?

Nobody knows everything about anyone. Grazia, for example, died of an exceptionally painful breast cancer. Which is what her first novel was about.

* * *

When time passes, does it leave anything behind? Doesn't everything move with it? Which means time never really passes, right? And me: am I ready to be a father? What do you think?

At the Portals of My Ears

At the Portals of My Ears

According to the television, certain ocean sponges have become carnivorous. Meanwhile, in Spirit Bay, Australia, others are being squeezed by benthic trawling. Ships drag nets across the sea floor, scooping indiscriminately. Interest groups have arisen. Lobbies. Sponge lovers worldwide are rallying!

I've just walked in to check on Henry. He's a different man to me today. Propped against the pillows, his breath heavy, he stares at the set. The tragedy of the sponge absorbs him. I, meanwhile, am getting used to the smell of shit, farts, the unpredictable seepage of fluids. For a minute, I too stare as the screen flashes images of the scrunchy brown and defenseless creatures. So many things in this world need protection, how will we possibly manage?

He coughs, then looks my way, a sly, familiar smile on his lips. "I need to get outta here for a while, kid." Pauses. "Up for a road trip?"

This I wasn't expecting.

"Serious, GF?" This is the man whose bedpan I emptied? Maybe he's trying to show me that he's still a man, no matter how badly he's been battered by the meteor shower of time. But what's that really mean anymore, being a man? Mom always said that was the world's whole problem in a word.

"Take a ride inside my life," he says in his bluff, lawyerly voice. "Feast on *my* past for a day! Nothing healthy about it, I promise."

Not like I have other plans. Before you know it, I'm pushing his wheel chair toward the open door of the black town car before which Werner stands waiting. Turns out the guy who helps Serafina get him in and out of bed at night is also his driver.

The morning's overcast. Clouds blot the sky. Any minute it will start to rain. Meanwhile the streets are always full of questions: that man with a black armband over his suit jacket— who died? That woman in the sari orange as a sunset: why is she in such a rush? The frizzy-haired girl dragging a dachshund, screaming at her phone. Why? Faces flick by faster than chat roulette. How many of these good folk go home, get naked, let the web cams roll? I'm guessing half. The new normal, my friends.

After Werner buckles down Henry's wheel chair, I slide in to the plush seat next to a minibar. "Where we heading?"

"I need to see some places. Just a feeling. Could be the last time, who knows?"

Around 57th St, we slow to a crawl. Henry asks: "You drive yet?"

"Next year."

"Right. Sorry. Stroke, you know." He struggles to raise his right arm, gets half-way up before it flops to his side. "Itchy. I'm itchy everywhere."

"Can I help?"

"Behind the right ear. If you wouldn't mind."

I lean over and scratch behind his ear the way I do with Rene's mother's doodle.

"I remember learning to drive. Old man taught me. Better

off doing it on my own. Even then I knew that, one day, I'd have a driver.

"He was a rough guy, my old man. Temper like you wouldn't believe. That's how it was with his generation. You hit your kid because you loved him. Teaching right from wrong. What mattered more? How to survive the world. Toughening me up, you know? Sometimes a belt was called for.

"Arrest you for that today."

He gazes into his lap. Rain blurs the windows. His voice softens.

"I remember once, I was seven, home from school for lunch, like always. A rainy day, like this. We had a rule that when it rained, you left your shoes outside the door. But I forgot. For some reason, Dad was home. He usually wasn't around days. Normally, he was at the store sixteen hours every day, six in the morning to ten at night. When he saw I was trekking puddles across the floor, he smacked the back of my neck so hard, I went flying forward and hit my head on a doorknob to the tune of four stitches. He worked hard for that varnish, that third floor unit in the green triple-decker a few blocks off Broad Street in Elizabeth. Nothing came free. An important lesson."

I watch a bicycle messenger swerve into a skid to avoid an opening door. His bike flies out from under him and nobody stops, like it happened on television. Henry just keeps talking.

"You could tell he didn't want to be that way, though. Look on his face when he hit me: you've never seen such a look. He couldn't help himself. That's the way he was. He always said that, 'That's just how I am.' Kind of like God, you know? *I am that I am.* Left that paradise first chance I got.

"But I've been thinking about it a lot lately. Wheelchair leaves you time to think, something I'd avoided all these years. There was always work, cases, girls."

A tour bus full of smiling strangers pulls up alongside. They're laughing and pointing and for a minute I wish I was up there with them.

"My old man's father was a coal miner, back in the old country. Came here planning for the mines but never got to Pennsylvania. Took a job on the docks in Elizabethport instead. My father started working in a grocery store around the corner at the age of twelve. By the time he was thirty, he owned it. A mom and pop place—until Mom left. Then it was just Pop. Take the Holland, Werner. But go through the Village."

"Down Broadway?"

"You know the way. I leave it to you."

A stalled bus slows us around Union Square. A long line of people waiting for some store to open wraps around the block. The rain falls steadily.

The Village is a place Mom talked about a lot when I was younger, but we never went.

"Help yourself to a coke."

"Want anything?"

"Dram of scotch be nice. Should be a bottle of Glenlivet somewhere there."

Way he tries not to look at me, I can tell he's embarrassed

about last night. I scan the row of smokey bottles, fill a glass.

"A straw?" Then: "That's the ticket."

Outside, an old woman with a rag moves from car to car in the rain, corn-rowed hair beaded with drops, water running down her face like tears, offering to wipe down windshields. Maybe more. When she approaches us, Werner lowers the window and slips her a twenty.

I take a deep breath.

"Listen, GF, I gotta ask you."

His mild grey eyes wipe over me.

"What was up with you and mom?"

"You found the letters. Of course." Looks at me, lips open loosely. Rain typing up a storm on the roof. "Maybe I hoped you would. Time was, Maddie and I wrote each other every day—even when one of us was napping in the other room."

I take this in while watching the old woman, who must be at least fifty (though, frankly, it's tough for me to figure out how old anybody over thirty really is) reach across a Miata's windshield. Then the traffic starts to move again.

We drive in silence as I try to make sense of a city that's always roiling like the inside of a volcano, everywhere life bubbling, hissing, bursting into flames, falling away, only to begin again.

"Your Dad and I lived near here once. Tompkins Square. Around the corner from where his mom grew up. Neighborhood wasn't so hip then. He must have told you." (He never talked about it.) "That's how we met: I answered his ad for a room-mate. I was a huge jazz and blues fan. Music scene was something else. The Fillmore, The Blue Note, Cafe au Go Go, The Bitter End, The Gaslight...

"Those days, I wasn't sure what I wanted to do. Only thing I knew, I wanted to make money. Saw what not having it did to my old man. I hadn't yet seen what having it did to those who did. Now I know. Law was a fall-back. Didn't have the balls, see, like your father. Took balls of steel to want to be a poet in those days.

"Took my first date to that club." His head gestures to a yellow awning painted over with initials I don't catch. "Her name was Janet Makluski. We took the bus from Elizabeth. You'll see. Know who we saw that night?"

"How could I, GF?"

He laughs. "Right. Just because we're here together, doesn't mean you know me. We're all just pretending we know each other. I'm saying, kid, we know squat. Squat.

"Sun House. Heard of him? No, right? Blues guy, way before your time. Janet was a poet, like your Dad. She kissed me on that corner there. 11:20, Friday night, October. We slowly made our way back to the bus station on 42nd, stopping to peer into windows and laughing at nothing at all. By the time we got to the station, the last bus had already left. We had no choice but to take a cab to Jersey. My heart was drumming the whole way back, because I knew. When we reached Janet's house, around 2 in the morning, I had to tell the cabbie I didn't have money for the fare. Janet had to wake her father for the dough. Walking home, to the other side of the city, I swore to myself that something like this would never happen to me again. Never spoke to Janet after that, though. And I still owe her old man $22."

On the corner stands a long-haired gent wearing a rain-streaked sandwich board that says: *Thank God You're Wrong!* and *Need a faith lift?* On the next corner, *Mattress Sale!*

I never had much religious education. Like I said before, Dad treated the bible like Bullfinch. He took *New Yorker* cartoons more seriously than God. But I gotta say, some things from that book stayed with me. Especially the Good Dude Jesus. The Good Dude Jesus was the kind of guy you wish could be your BFF, so long as he didn't get into your shit *too* much. And not only because he could supersize your 'za. He liked the ladies. I remember that.

"Know what I regret most?" He continued, eyes roaming the avenue. We're threading narrow streets like in some movie from another century, past windows hawking high-end clothes and hookahs, serene stone Buddhas, vape shops, nouveau smores.

"When I got that scholarship, I was outta the house, and never looked back. Said, the hell with these people. Who are they to me? Right? I hate myself for it today. Go up 8th Street, Werner.

"My mother was long gone. The rest of the family seemed like a hostile tribe.

"Old man was a bastard, but he was there, I'll give him that. Never remarried either. Just wasn't room for two men in the house, though. He never left it. Died alone, on Halloween, watching Johnny Carson."

His soft voice drops. He gestures at the window with his head.

"Know what used to be on 8th Street? Wilentz's 8th Street Bookstore. Your father haunted the place. Dragged me along. Nah, I was glad to go. They had these racks on the second floor, at the front of the store near the windows. Kind you used to see in every drugstore, stocked with romances, thrillers, that kind of thing. Only, these held something different. Literary magazines. Our favorite being *Fuck You: A Magazine of the Arts.*

"But your father. He just dug into his poetry foxhole and wouldn't leave. He was gonna make it if it killed him. Or me, or you. You know he used to dress up before sitting down to write? Tells you something, doesn't it?

"He ever talk to you about *his* father?"

"I knew him," I said, remembering our visits to the pseudo-corpse reposing at Mt. Auburn Hospital, where Dad would ditch me and dash out.

"Your grandfather was the meanest motherfucker I'd ever met. He was a cold mean. Money-mean. Made my old man look like Mr. Rogers. Sooner smack me upside the head than put me in the hands of someone who feels nothing, and acts like you're not there. You got more vibe off a brick than from that prick." He sighs. I'm touched by how much he feels for Dad.

I keep looking for an opening so I can tell him about Rene and our situation but he just prattles on. It's so unlike GF to reminisce, I keep it zipped.

"I remember when this was *the Bowery*. Drunks propped these buildings up like faith. Hundreds lined the street, not long ago."

"Now your grandmother, that's another story. She was the sweetest Slavic lady. And I mean lady, in the old-fashioned sense. She grew up not far from here, in Alphabet City. All the virtues: pretty, thrifty, loved working with her hands. Always embroidering, sewing, stewing, pickling. The heart of the house: Anna. Thrifty even in her name. Two letters, repeated. Sooner choke on a bone than complain.

"With her accent, everything she said sounded like singing. That's where your father got his confidence. She gave him the nerve he needed to keep on. Shit a brick if she wasn't the sweetest woman who ever lived. Died young.

"You have to understand: Your father was a phenom. Glad the world finally saw it.

"All right, let's blow this fire trap. Werner, Jersey!"

* * *

As the car slips underground, he sighs: "Still get nervous in a tunnel. River above us, believe it? Five million cars pass through here every year. A miracle it's not been bombed, or sprung a leak. Who taught you to drive?"

"I don't. You tried once, a few years back. Remember?"

"Did I? Oh, yeah. I remember now. Didn't go so well, did it?"

"I crashed your car."

"A learning experience."

After the tunnel, it's another planet. A knot of highways segmented by pink swamps. Routes criss-cross like a schizo's etcha-sketcha. The beauty of industrial pollution: stalagmites of steel, a galaxy of headlights spinning wild. Flamingos in the marshes: real? Plastic? What's the diff? For all I know, Jersey may well be the last best breeding ground for pink flamingoes. And everyone speeding, speeding to—or from—the fire of their lives.

Three streams of traffic flowing fast and rough. Turnpike to Route 22, with its endless muffler repair shops, gas stations, dollar stores, strip clubs.

"Question you ask at my age," Henry goes on: "Are you where you *had* to be? Was it fate, or choices *you* made, led you here, to this limo, beside a middle-aged man in a wheel chair, talking wet? I'll take another," he nods at his glass. "Against the grain," he adds. "Always best to go against the grain. People don't seem to get that."

He's on his third Glenlivet.

"Sorry I've been such a lousy godfather. There's no script for the part—unless you're Marlon Brando." Checks to make sure I got the reference. "At some point, if you're lucky, you get busy. Work. Women. Or men. Or whatever. And the other little diversions you devise along the way—golf, video games, gambling. Now gambling's something I can get behind.

"Hillside to Broad, Werner. Be a right, a mile up."

"You've been great, GF," I say. "That's why I'm here."

We turn off 22. We're nosing down Broad Street, where

it's lunchtime and the streets are swarmed by zombies hunting for a limb. The rain too seems on break.

Henry's grey eyes gaze at me with a sadness I've not seen in them before.

"Tough about your parents. I always wondered when your old man would act out who he really was. Took a while. Hard for you, I know. My parents split when I was ten.

"When my mother left us, I knew why. The old man was more than anyone should put up with, no doubt about that. Killed me for a while that she'd leave me with him, though. I couldn't blame her, but in my heart I did. Oh boy did I blame her. I blame her still."

Which is interesting to hear, that stuff can last that long, and can keep happening in your head. Makes me even more pissed at Dad. And it leaves me wanting to take better care with what I do today.

"Welcome to Elizabeth, my friend, where it began for me." He sounds brighter, cheery even, more awake. "Used to be a Gimbels on this corner, a Levi's there. That's the Army Navy store where I bought my first bell bottoms. The Presbyterian Church. City Hall. The Regent movie theater's now Zarah's Furniture. George Washington sailed to his inauguration in Manhattan from here. A girl once told me she was glad I lived inside a woman's name."

"Down Grier. Slower. Here, stop here a minute. That house there?" Pointing at a brown triple decker behind a chain-link fence, a pale blue and pink Madonna in a shell in on the long front lawn. "That's where Tamara lived. Tamara was my first great love. She came after Janet. I'd have done anything for her. Problem is, she knew it. There are people, once they know they got you, they no longer want you. That was the dance we danced. First she broke my heart, doesn't matter how. We got over it. Then, when I knew she was completely mine, I dumped her. Didn't mean to; hadn't been my plan. Just seemed to happen on its own. After, I swore I'd never care so much again.

"And then I met your mother. And everything that followed was because of what didn't work out between us."

He shuts his eyes. Then he turns and looks at me so intensely it scares me.

"Your mother and I were close once, yes. When she was in college. Your father was her TA. One night, she joined us for drinks at the White Horse. Long before your old man made a move—and now maybe we know why he took his time—she and I began seeing each other. But she kept talking about him. The more she talked about him, the more I wanted her. She was a wild child. One of those Jewish girls whose parents started out working in the garment district, and wound up rich, but kept their communist ideas they passed on to their kids. Madeline, with her Janis Joplin hair, her radical priests, South American poetry, the Black Panthers. She was burning. She was fire. She was right. She was the fire next time. I wanted her. Man, did I want her.

"But she was crazy. She liked to drive with her eyes closed. Nearly got us killed, too. One summer morning, about a month after we began seeing each other, she said she wanted to go to the shore. She didn't have a car. I had an old, red Karmann Ghia my mother's brother sold me cheap when I graduated high school. He felt bad about his sister abandoning us the way she did. Must have been fifteen years old, but a beauty.

"For us, the shore meant Sandy Hook, where the surf was like a perfect roller coaster. Your mother insisted she wanted to drive. She knew I'd do anything she asked. She didn't drive, had never taken a lesson, but I didn't know that. It hadn't come up. I asked her to be careful with my baby. She laughed that throaty smoker's laugh. We never made it out of the city. We were in the Holland Tunnel when we slammed the station wagon in front of us. She said the tunnel scared her, so she put pedal to metal and roared in, eyes shut. That was the end of that car. I didn't care. If that was what she wanted, all right then. And that was my mistake."

It's not hard for me to imagine Mom doing something like this. What's confusing is trying to figure out what any of it has to do with me.

"You must have gotten your driving chops from her.

"But your father was a poet, and for some reason this made Madeline believe he saw the world like she did. She ditched me to be with him. She pursued him. Wasn't long after they married that she found he didn't share the reckless aspirations of a dreamy rich girl from the Bronx. Even as a student, she was always volunteering for some blood-soaked mission. She went to El Salvador, Chile, Guatemala. Your father, meanwhile, had only one thing on his mind: his career. He was going to succeed as a poet if it killed him, and/or anyone in his way. That was when she got back in touch with me.

"She was my last great love. I had no others after her; only wives and girlfriends." He twists his neck side to side.

"Need me to scratch you again?"

"That's all right. Look, Jonathan, most people don't know who they are. Your father knew a lot. But I think he was so afraid of his old man, even after he was dead, that he couldn't cop to it. Some people are like that. Better for everyone if your mom had stayed with me."

When he tells me this, I think of my other favorite book, after the *Memoirs of an Anarchist*. It's called *The Wanderer*, by this French guy, Alain-Fournier, who died in the first World War. It's about this kid everybody calls the Great Meaulnes, who runs away from school and gets lost in the countryside. There he accidentally stumbles on a costume party for kids at some great estate where he meets a girl named Yvonne and falls insanely in love with her. Later, though, he can't find the house again. It's like he dreamed it, like it was Camelot. A lot of other stuff happens, and of course, in the end, she dies.

All this time we're parked in front of that dumpy triple-decker. Suddenly Henry says:

"Oh my god."

At that moment the door of the house opens and a out steps a woman in a tan rain coat. She wears black rubber boots and carries a red umbrella. Even from a distance I can tell she's really thin. Too thin. Sick thin.

Henry tenses. The heel of his hand lands clumsily on the

button that rolls down the window. The woman has locked the door and walks quickly down the damp-stained path toward the gate. My eyes move from my godfather to her.

Latching the gate behind her, she can't help noticing the town car, window open on its two passengers, one a man in a wheel chair, staring open-mouthed, the other a long-haired kid, also looking her way. It's no surprise she turns and begins walking quickly down the street.

"Tamara," Henry cries, softly at first, then louder, "Tamara!"

The woman stops. She turns, and when she does, I see her face clearly for the first time. It's the face of a dark bird, a magpie or a crow: black hair badly dyed, nose long and thin, hooked sharply at the end, chin like a trowel.

"Yes. That's me. Can I help you?"

I can tell the GF's surprised—that she'd heard him, that she'd stopped, that she'd turned—and also a little embarrassed, and uneasy. Like, what's he say to her now?

The woman stands her ground and Henry's forced to lean sideways in the chair so that his head is almost sticking out the window. He shouts "It's Henry, Tam, Henry Pontopiddan."

It takes a minute for the name to sink in. But when it does, I see her face change, relax a little. She comes up to the window.

"Jesus H. Christ. Henry! Well, pass the ammunition. Damn."

After that, she seems unsure what to say. The wheel chair's clearly visible. Does she ask about it? Say nothing?

"How the hell are you, Henry?"

"I'm okay," he says. "I'm okay."

It's what people will say to each other even as wild dogs tear apart their limbs. How are you? Oh, I'm okay, I guess.

"How are you? You look great."

"Oh, well." She's struggling to decide how much to say. "Henry, it's so strange to see you." I give her points for not saying it was wonderful, but her hesitation seems to make the GF even more uncomfortable.

There's a silence, then she speaks again: "Henry, I can't talk now. My kid's sick. I'm on my way to see her. She's at the hospital. She's waiting for me."

"Can I give you lift?"

"Thanks, that's sweet. Really, thanks. But it's just a block away. Remember? St. Elizabeth's?"

"Is she all right?"

"Oh, Henry," the woman suddenly tears up. Then she says: "I have to go."

And she turns and hurries off.

We sit in silence so long I think my head's about to explode.

When the rain starts up again, the GF finally speaks:

"OK, Werner. Parkway. Atlantic City. Let's have some fun."

* * *

Three in the afternoon, I'm inside Drumbkopf's Doge Palace Casino's VIP Room, sipping coke while Henry purrs under a lap dance from a blond with breasts hand-made by gods. Werner sits beside me, working his iPhone. Wonder if he's tweeted our whereabouts.

I'm still shaking from our last encounter which, I kid you not, was with a lion with a human face.

After his fifth tumbler of Glenlivet, the GF started to unravel. As we approached Atlantic City, he began telling me about his ex-wives, his women friends, none of whom have called him since his stroke, and how he's given up on that. He talked about an elephant named Lucy we could visit down in Margate later, and how his lucky number was 4-7-6, which was the year Rome fell. I was right not to have mentioned anything about Rene.

He said: "People will tell you about fate and karma, thinking they know how things happen, one thing causing another, but I'm telling you they don't know shit. The race is rarely to the swift. Accident. Luck. You roll the dice. Time and chance upend us all! Atlantic City is America's Jerusalem, our Mecca. Here you see how world systems *really* work."

When we arrived at the casino, some guy in a shiny rich brown suit came right up to us, crying "Henry! Been a long time! Great to see you!" He reached to shake the GF's hand. "Oh, sorry, right. I heard about the stroke. Glad you made it anyway. Your room is always ready. Any bags?"

Then: "Anything you'd like to see? Our magic show's about to start in the Drumbkopf Coliseum. One flight down."

That's where we head. An elevator drops us underground, then a hallway, where we fall in line with the crowd, some of whom wear nothing more than robes and flip flops. Nobody blinks at a kid strolling beside a man in a wheel chair pushed by a guy with a mohawk and leather pants. We pass through two sets of sliding doors, until we reach our destination, with its painted porticoes and columns. Between the Doge Palace and it, I wonder what this mash-up of Italian imperial history is saying.

I've visited the real thing in Rome, where they fed Christians to the lions (fact or urban legend?), and it's bigger by a mile, and full of rats, and rabid dogs. Or so Dad said. Luckily, these seats are sewn in velvet and not stone.

An usher in a toga steers us to the front row, aisle, so Henry doesn't have to leave his wheel-chair. The place is full. I hear the breathing of the crowd, smell the buttered popcorn. The rising background music's vintage, by a local: Springsteen. "Born to Run."

The lights go out, the music swells until it's all we know. Then, on a dime, a silence falls like sudden death—or maybe we've gone deaf? Before us, floating in mid-air's a bearded man in a purple jacket, waving his icicle-like wand our way.

Before you know it, we're all rising, first it's inches, then it's almost a foot. It seems the cushions of our seats are hovercrafts. Way cool; and then we're spinning. I glance down at the

GF, who's missing all the fun. He's smiling. Seconds later, we land softly, as our Houdini also touches ground. Mere minutes in, we're at his mercy.

For the next hour, his tricks hold us like a dream. There's a story threading through, something corny, about a girl who's lost somewhere in hell, a lover scouring the cosmos, scrubbing every black hole in the universe, against a backdrop of a sky the Hayden Planeterium must envy. Along the way he slays warlocks, wizards, demons, dragons, and a little boy who nearly takes him down, until our hero catches on: that kid's himself, from long ago, who, as a child did something he should not have, and his sin, compounded over time, now threatens to destroy him. Meanwhile, the mouth of hell has opened. Out rush monsters like you've never seen from Pixar, only each of these reflects your face: your eyes, your nose, your teeth are lunging at you on the body of a lion, and just when you're about to shit your pants, the lights go on. Show's done.

No wonder afterwards the bars are packed.

Walking back through the slot parlor, Henry says to Werner, "Show him." We stop before a slot that's just been vacated. Werner grabs the stool top with both hands and yanks upward. It pops off like a bottle top. He then reaches under the slot machine itself and pulls out a fresh cushion which he slaps onto the stand. He turns to me and grins like he's solved Rubik's cube.

"So?" I ask, not understanding what I'm being shown.

"Tell him," Henry says.

"See those people standing there?"

He points to a row of men and women, mostly old and scruffy-looking, hanging on the fringes of the hall.

"They call them vultures. They're waiting for one of these good people," he gestures at the crowds gaping intently at the spinning icons in the little windows.

"For what?"

"For them to leave. They know that, sooner or later, these machines pay off. So they watch to see who's stuck it out the longest before finally giving up. Then they start to play. Never know when the next spin will score."

"What's that got to do with the seats?"

"I'll tell you. The regulars who sit here know the game. They know if they play long enough, and lose enough money, they will, eventually, get at least some of it back, so they refuse to leave until they win. When nature calls, they answer it right here. Most come wearing diapers. Sometimes, though, that's not enough. Seats get stained. What's a little dignity against the risk of being called a chump?

"In order not to let a slot stay down for more than a few seconds, the Casino has this way of making it all nice. That's in addition to pumping extra oxygen into the room.

"Breathe deep. Pretend you've climbed a mountain."

* * *

In the VIP Room, the girls are working. My eyes are popping while Werner hardly seems to notice. He's fixated on his iPhone.

"Watcha doing?" I finally ask.

"*Resident Evil,*" he answers without glancing up.

I turn to see that Henry's napping, though the girl is grinding down his beans the best she can.

The light show is fantastic. You almost feel the different colors pulse along your skin: purple, orange, and green.

So far, nobody's tried carding me, and I've had to say no thank you to some babes I thought lived only on the web, or in my head. In the flesh, they're scarier than Dad. Amazing. Both.

* * *

Henry finally passes out in his chair. The girl who'd been in his lap melts away, leaving in her wake a frail, silver-feathered husk, snoring like a baby, spittle on his chin.

"Well that was quick," says Werner. "Ready to go home?"

Half-way up the Turnpike, Henry wakes. Swivels, blank-faced, stoned.

"It's cool, GF. We're going home."

And then he starts to cry. His hoarse voice whispers, "Kill me. Kill me." He hangs his head, arms drooping from his sides.

"It's okay," I tell him. I look out the window, at the head-lights racing through the dark. All I can think of is Beyah. I need to see her. These old folk will be the death of me.

Rabindranath Tagore, Poet, 1861-1941

Our subject Rabindranath was a poet, of course, as well as a supporter of the Indian independence party. First non-Westerner to win the Nobel Prize (1913). *He* dubbed Gandhi Mahatma. Meaning *The Great One*. According to Mom, somebody once asked Gandhi what he thought of Western Civ and he said: "It would be a good idea." Even so, I saw on television that in India you can buy a kidney for about 15 grand; a heart for 120. Rabindranath wrote: "I have spent my days in stringing and unstringing my instruments." I have spent mine pondering that brain teaser. So far, *nichts*.

Tagore began writing poems at eight. He published his first book at sixteen. (Sorry, Dad.) Wrote national anthems for both India and Bangladesh, which I just downloaded for inspiration. He too mainly skipped school and was educated at home, often by his servants, while roaming the grounds around his mansion. His mother died when he was young; and his father was on the road a lot. His ancestors basically founded their own religion, so you might say God was his playmate. It was the first casteless movement in India. No creeds, sacred texts, or priests. Everything that lives is holy. There is no heaven but what you find here, and yet the soul survives forever. These things get tricky in the execution, I imagine. Because of their unpopular beliefs, nobody wanted to marry into the family, so the Tagores wed each other. When I imagine marrying Asia, I feel like throwing up. Maybe you get used to it.

Tagore was knighted in 1915. In 1919, after a massacre of Indians by the Brits, he gave the knighthood back. I've never heard of anyone returning a prize. Just not done anymore, I guess.

Here's one last bit from RT: "My poet, is it thy delight to see thy creation through my eyes and to stand at the portals of my ears to listen to thy eternal harmony?"

In this case, the Ramones.

* * *

By the time we get back to New York, it's nearly ten. While Henry slept the entire way, I thought about my next move.

I know it doesn't make any sense, but I just have to see Beyah again. Maybe it's all the strippers falling over Henry. Maybe it's his story about my mother, his lost love, and how everything went south after that. I gotta choice to make here soon. How do I know it will be the right one?

If I do go see her, what will we talk about? But that's easy: girls like to talk about themselves. They love it when you ask them questions—about their families, especially their mothers, their friends, etc. Best of all is when you ask them how they're feeling. Usually they're feeling awful to start, but after three or four hours of blah blah blah, they're miraculously better. You, meanwhile, are ready to eat a grenade.

I wait until Werner's put Henry to bed and said good night. There's still no sign of Serafina, but I know where I need to go.

* * *

Near midnight, sweating like a motherfucker, I'm at the Adirondacks Trailways terminal at Port Authority, using Mom's credit card for a round trip to Kingstown.

At this hour, we slip out of the city easy as a morning fart. At some point, I doze. In my dream, Rene is crying. I wake up in a sweat. The world's a blur of trees and, beyond them, the first small fists of mountains. No traffic at all as we pull into town. Four a.m., and Kingstown is Deadsville. The depot's housed at a gas station on Washington Avenue.

I'm alone off the bus, which goes on to Albany.

Asked yesterday where I'd be today, I'd have said the Park, the pad, or trouble. Instead, I'm staking out the pre-dawn streets with my size tens. Black. How come these houses huddled close exhale a gust of wilderness? I no sooner think this than I hear Rene's voice over my shoulder. When I whirl around, nada. Most of the lamps are out. The only earthly glow comes from the little store in the gas station. Then my eyes rove up, and what? What otherwise I never see: a sky ablaze with stars. Who ever knew there were so many? I turn and head for the store.

A grizzly of a girl behind the gas station's tiny counter vacuums air with her mouth open. I look around: Walmart in a few square feet. Two hundred of everything: chewing gum, candy bars, power drinks, fishing gear, ammo in loose shells and clips, night crawlers, ice cream, shoe polish, more ice cream, cereal, air-fresheners, cigarettes, nasal sprays, key chains, lighters, magazines (*Hustler* and *Swank* behind the counter), and more ice cream. Two hundred kinds of rubbers, too. I've never used one—Rene claimed to be on the pill.

The woman eyes me like I might be packing. Lights a clove cigarette.

"'Scuse me, ma'am, you know where I might find The Portuguese Pines?"

"The Pines?" Voice uneasy under humming lights. "Used to have only resort-type places. Everybody came then. Kids from the city. Each year I'd catch some sticking candy down their pants. They think fat makes you blind," she says, "they do it right in front of me. I'm watchin', they're stuffin'. Today almost nobody comes. 'Sept 'em Portos." She sweeps a rag off the counter and wipes her face with it. I space out while she's goes light speed, getting into it...

"...straight down this street til you get to the end of the Kmart parking lot where you make a left. Probably see Morton. Harmless. Lives in a car. Army suit's the only clothes he wears since getting back but we remember him when he was just a brat, so we don't mind..."

...on and on she goes, but for whatever reason I hear little and remember less. Keep going is about all I take in of her good counsel. She's sluttier and more foul-looking by the second and I have to keep myself from hitting on her. Then I see a dog without a nose curled beside the counter watching me. "What's with Rover," I ask.

"Coyotes," she snaps. "Go after you there's enough of 'em and they're hungry. Say it's global warming, but I ain't buyin' it. Winter before last blew out my snow-blower."

So this is the America of which Dad speaks with such panic. Coyotes or no coyotes, I know where I want to be. Now I know how to get there. I thank the woman extravagantly, praise her store like it was Bloomies, and buy the biggest item I can find, which turns out to be a fishing rod I'll never use (the car battery makes no sense). I swipe Mom's credit card through the machine, scribble my mark, and set off. Outside, I lean the fishing rod, still in its package, against a gas pump, and head down the street. Past the Kmart—no sign of whatshisname—I enter a residential neighborhood. Must be garbage day. Street's lined with bins heaped with newspapers and bottles next to discarded appliances. A gang of raccoons pick over a bag whose guts splatter the street. They barely look up when I pass. Instinctively I reach for my phone. Not in this pocket. Or that. Fuck. I frisk myself. Must have fallen out on the bus. May be the first time in my life without it. Doublefuck.

Into the darkness I push. To put it strangely. And the dark doth thicken. I lean into the hill. Houses thin out. Soon it's hard to tell where the garbage gives way to domestic debris. Lit by what looks like a kerosene lamp in the window (or maybe the house is on fire), I see a bathtub, a plaster gnome without a head, hundreds of tires.

Now the houses disappear entirely. As the paving ends, I step onto a dirt road and enter a tunnel of trees. So dark I can't see my own hand. Might as well be blind. Still I keep moving. The black-leafed branches rustle. Wind; wolves. Why, I wonder, do we even have countryside? Why haven't we paved it over? What purpose does it serve? From what I've just heard, it's filled with nothing but horrors. I'm scaring myself. All I need is to keep walking this road to the top of the hill, where I'll see a big sign saying *Portuguese Pines*. That much I heard the fat lady say. Haven't I, a million times, set off not knowing where? And have I ever seen the trace of a tiger or a terrorist? Not one pickpocket have I encountered. Hopped into cars, trains, planes, even buses: each uncertain step an act of faith. But this wilderness is a different world. Snakes pumping cytoxic venom, machete-wielding survivalists. These are real.

It's gotten warmer and more humid. A night the moon seems hotter than the sun. Beads of sweat blur my vision. Still I go on. Stop. Think. Stopthink. But the demons in my brain swing chainsaws with abandon.

Then the howl. Coyotes! *That's* what is out there. I see my bleached skull on the cover of The Enquirer: *Urban Songwriter Devoured by Coyots!* Fortunately the cry comes from behind and below: turning back leads to the jaws of death. Onward!

I'm sweating worse now. The fringes of night are beginning to gray. Silvery hairs of dawn fall, one here one there. My mood is lifting. Dear daylight, come to save me. And then I see it: the hilltop.

Tired, I slump down below the sign. *Portuguese Pines.* The Catskills, New York. I lean against a tree and drift away. Still the howls come, loud, and louder.

Melvin Tolson, poet, 1898-1966

Melvin graduated with honors from Lincoln University, Pa., in 1922, the year T.S. Eliot published *The Waste Land* in *The New Criterion,* a magazine Eliot himself edited. Dad says this is common as cow shit. Dad edited a magazine too until he got bored reading other people's work. Now he reads his own poems almost exclusively. (Kidding, Dad. You're a genius.) In 1930-31, Tolson did an M.A. at Columbia, where he wrote a thesis on the poets of the Harlem Renaissance. Meanwhile the dust bowl rolled on. After graduating, he moved to Marshall, Texas, with his wife, where he taught speech and English at Wiley College. *Dark Symphony* appeared in the *Atlantic Monthly* in 1941. Dad bitches that he can't get published in that rag. Why he cares I've no idea.

Though he was born in Moberly, Missouri, Melvin Tolson became poet laureate of Liberia in 1947. His dad was a Methodist minister, son of a slave and her white master. In 1953, Melvin finished his epic poem in honor of the nation's centennial, *Libretto for the Republic of Liberia.* He then returned to the United States, where he served as mayor of Langston, Oklahoma, from 1954 to 1960. Here he was accused of helping farm laborers and tenant farmers to organize. Denzel plays him in a movie called *The Great Debaters,* which I haven't seen.

* * *

Dawn. Come round again. Damn. Does the world really turn? Klyt has doubts. I rub eyes gummed with sleep. Woody pleads for mercy. *Calma calma* I whisper. Not exactly our living room. Different shades of green cover the earth. Shiver in the chill, wet grass. I breathe a freshness like the inside of an orange and feel the green below my skin. Rise, stretch, and see the banner behind me: *Welcome to Portuguese Pines!* Is there such a thing, I wonder, as a Portuguese pine? Probably not.

Tractor manned by a dude in a piss-yellow wife-beater and backwards cap slow-storms the hill. I sneeze, brush grass off jeans and hoodie. "Yo," I shout. He hears nothing. Sucking smoke takes concentration. He's passing me so I start jumping up and waving until he stops. Engine drops to a grumble. Dude rises. Big fella.

"By any chance know a chick named Beyah?" I holler.

Eyes squint like he's unsure whether to spit, speak, or shoot. "Who you?" he asks.

"Call me Smedley."

"Smedley, hunh? What you doin' here, kid?"

"Looking for Beyah."

He keeps squinting. Fingers a belt loop, leaning back to adjust his sights. "How come you lookin' for Beyah?"

So she is here, I think. "She's an old friend. From school."

He scratches under his arm, rubs his nose with the back of his hand, and picks up a tallboy of Colt 45. "School, hunh?"

"Since third grade." I consider adding that I'm no cop, but why give the man ideas? Finally he shrugs:

"Yeah, she's here. Get on." He chucks the empty can into the woods. Sits back down while I scramble up.

Beyond the trees rise odd-looking houses and barracks. Two boys struggle with a volleyball net. A mixed group kick around a soccer ball. A summer camp. Then I hear a shot and suddenly I'm nervous, like I've crossed a border without proper papers. A steroid trauma struts for the woods clutching a crossbow.

We pull up before an outdoor mess hall. Twenty or so people—more kids than grown-ups—sit at tables on the concrete platform below an orange awning. The air fills with the smells of outdoor fire, bacon, frying potatoes, bread.

"Jonathan! What are you doing here?"

From the blur of the crowd, she swells up. Pink bikini top, denim shorts, red flip flops.

"Thought you said your name's Smedley." My driver pops another Colt.

I ignore everything except *her*.

Her face reddens. She stares at the ground. Curls like copper shavings covering bare shoulders in the rising light. The sun spills over the trees and I begin to sweat. She moves toward me anyway and when she gets here, she offers me her hand. I hold my breath before taking it because I know a million volts are about to pass through me. They do. Somehow I survive.

Suddenly I feel self-conscious. Voices break the sound barrier with a mix of Porto and English. I'm ashamed at having none of this fine Romance language in my repertoire. Another sign our educational institutions don't know shit. How many even offer Portuguese on the menu? Mom's credit card may have just enough left for the Rosetta Stone DVDs. But something's not right. I feel it.

We stand in a silence all our own. What is there to say? What I've done by showing up here after speaking with this girl for fifteen minutes yesterday—was it really only yesterday, or was it the day before?—is either insane or prophetic. She'd be well within her rights to call the cops or send her older cousins or whoever these cats be—two fat bruisers I saw lugging stones to a wall along the road—to kick me out. Or put a bullet in the back of my head. The crazy part is I don't know if I'm here to ask her to run away with me or explain why I can't. You'd think a guy would know such things already.

We stand so close, I feel her exhalations on my cheek. Around us, people stare. I ignore them, concentrating on what I'll say next.

"Café de Manha?" she asks.

"Sure," I say.

Beyah hands me a paper plate and fork and leads me to a spread which reminds me I'm starved. She points to what looks like French toast made from French bread: rabanada. "Pao de Queijo, bolo de fuba, black beans, flan...." she recites down the line. I heap my plate with eggs and breads and beans while she settles for the coffee and some kind of sweet roll and we go to a long table where we join half a dozen chattering kids. They don't look at me. I'm alone in the cone of silence with Beyah.

It's a silence neither of us breaks. I'm confused, tired, and psyched out of my skull. Did I mention she's wearing hardly any clothes? A pink bikini top. Most of the others girls here are also bounteous babes similarly attired. Yet even in this crowd, Beyah shines like she swallowed a star.

A voice from the table behind us shouts something in Portuguese. Beyah keeps her eyes on her mug. The voice rises again. She turns and snaps back angrily.

I seem to have put her in a situation. I shovel down the eggs and think: what do I have to offer? Two parents who hate each other, a little sister who feels betrayed, and a stroke-paralyzed godfather?

And what about Rene? I love Rene. What am I doing here? I frisk myself, searching for my lost cell phone.

Finally, Beyah, says: "My uncles own this place. My mother's brothers. Those are my brothers and sisters over there," she points to a group arranged like Russian dolls at a table on the other side of the dining hall. "The others are mainly people from the parish. Some cousins."

I look at the crew, suddenly silent. They glare back.

"My uncle called and asked if we could come up early to help out. My mom has hardly been home in months," she adds. "That's why I came the other day. Can't count on Moma."

"I know exactly what you mean," I say. Then I tell her about Mom and Dad: how Dad used to be a good guy when we were kids, how he got caught up in this po-biz racket, how he kept looking for jobs, and when he finally landed one that seemed great, he began getting stranger and stranger. And now this. (Of course, the stories Henry told me complicate the picture.)

She listens, nodding. That she hasn't yet said *leave* inspires me. I tell her I hate him. I explain how I got myself suspended and that I will never to return to school. I'll stay with GF and become a writer.

"How old are you, Mr. Hemingway?" she asks.

"Fifteen," I say.

Nods again, like I'm telling her nothing new. Awful lot of nodding going on.

"I bet you're a great writer."

The way she says it, I expect her to reach over and pat me on the head.

I shrug. But I can think of nothing more to say to this sinuous, frizzy-haired, dark-skinned dakini across the table.

"You finished? Let's walk," she says. "There's a lake behind the trees."

The sun's heating up fast. The grass has dried. My forehead beads like an abacus. The others are still eating. Some wave to Beyah as we leave the dining area. One dude winks and she flips him the bird. We pass wooden bungalows like dwarf houses and rows of tents, to a little patch of woods. At its edge, we pause. Beyah points to several large wooden crates on stilts. I hear buzzing fifty feet away. "Ernesto's hives," she says. "One of my uncles. Next week, the kids start coming up on weekends. When school's done, place gets mobbed."

"Cool. You all stay here too?"

"We're gonna this year, after school's out for the kids."

"Right." But what I see is Serafina rushing through the Park when she was supposed to be at the apartment, and lying to me about where she goes, and what's worse, deceiving Beyah.

"Why does your mom say you're still in Brazil?"

"If you really want to know, *meu pai's* on Riker's," she blurts.

Riker's, I know, is a prison.

The etiquette of jail I learned from hanging around Astro, Mom, and GF; main thing is, it's their stuff, you have to let them tell it when they want.

"He's from Valdares. Crossed the border twenty years ago. No papers."

I nod.

"Back then, there was nothing there, no work, no future. He wanted to help his parents. Wanted to build them a house. So he crossed an invisible line."

"Your mother too?" Suddenly I worry the GF might get in trouble.

Turns out, her mother was born here. Her father got here twenty years ago. Soon after he left Valdares, things back home got better while all hell broke loose here. They bought a house in Jersey, on a block where half the other houses were abandoned. Then he lost his job, and suddenly they couldn't make their payments. Everything started to go bad. Her parents fought. Her father began to drink. Her brothers got into trouble in school. A year ago, her father was stopped for driving with a busted brake light. He's been in jail ever since. Her mother, who worked for the GF for years, turned to him for help. Then he had his stroke. Because some people are just born lucky.

When the tears start, there's no slowing them. What can I possibly know? What can I understand of her sitch? She sees how the GF lives—the pad, the art, the girls....How could I know what it feels like to know that any minute everything you care most about—parents, siblings, friends—can disappear? That ICE—ICE!—can show up at your door, at your school, at your job, and take you or your father away. Don't I see her life's impossible? The kids, her mother, and now her father in jail, and about to be deported? GF has been their only friend, he was going to get her father out, now look at him.

She stands there sobbing not three feet away and I can't move.

After a few minutes, during which I wish I could hide in a cave for a decade, she finally says: "Let's walk."

We walk through a stand of pines to where the bluest lake in the world awaits. Soon her tears dry; she's smiling again. A breeze nipples the water. I have always wanted to use that word as a verb.

Wind sets the high tension wires of her hair trembling. I glance at her: Water and sky mass in her eyes. Her forehead and cheeks dazzle with sweat. Her breasts. I mean it. Just period. Her belly shimmers with a sheen of oil. I want to fall through the earth to the burning core. She smiles like she can read my thoughts. It is, at the same time, an awkward and uncertain smile. Everything's so still, I hear salamanders rustling in the leaves. Turtles tap-dance underwater, mushrooms soar skyward, and the sound of a star dying alone in a galaxy billions of miles away.

Not really, but you know what I mean.

"It's been a long time since anybody went this crazy over me," she says, sounding more flattered than pissed. "It's very sweet you found me."

Yes, I think, but I have no idea what to do with you now that I have. Because there's Rene—but I can't bring myself to say anything. Maybe I should just start over. Become a fisherman, a gun-runner, a monk. Suddenly I feel a sharp pain rush through my chest.

"I'll always remember this," she begins. "Really. You have to believe me. The way the lake looks. How your hands are shaking." (I squeeze them into fists and shut my eyes, because she's making fun of me, and because I know what's coming). "You can always be my friend…"

I open my eyes again. I talk too much when I get nervous except when I get really nervous and then I can't talk at all.

She sighs, gives me a look. It's the gaze of someone much older. Maybe thirty. Who knows things I might never. Her face is written in a foreign script, lines on her forehead spell nights of long sighs.

…and then she steps forward and her soft hands land on either cheek as she brings my head down toward her and places one kiss on each wet lid. Then raises it back, saying:

"Open your eyes, Jonathan. Nothing's easy for me."

She pauses with her mouth open as though the last long *e* did her in. Somewhere, a cloud shivers. Maybe.

"If this was earlier. If we met sooner. A month ago. I was free then. But, now, Albert and I... He's here..."

My fists clench again, shoulders jerk. Her hand seizes my chin. She turns my head. Our eyes lock. Then our foreheads kiss. We stay like that for several minutes as something passes through us, and I melt away.

Because we're all just atoms whirling, only that, and nothing more.

And then I'm turning away, walking into trees, kicking them, saying fuck fuck and she says not a word, and the back of her hand at her mouth.

When I open my eyes, I half expect to find night fallen. Instead, the light floods in, blinding me. This is how it must be, I tell myself. This is how it must be. I will never love another for the rest of my days. I will die with the name Beyah on my lips, and she will never know.

And when she's old and gray, one morning she'll open her eyes and look out the window of her bleak little room in the nursing home and she'll remember me, and this morning. She'll cough, cross ancient feet with their painted toenails in red flip flops, and let the curtain drop. She'll sink into her wheelchair, light a cigarette, and stare down at the floor. She'll be alone, of course. And a trifle asthmatic...

Then something smacks me in the back of my neck. I whirl to see the beanie bag hit the ground, and three brats, nine, ten, who knows, pointing fingers, and I look over my shoulder and

Beyah's laughing with her sibs that I'd drown like cats, given the chance.

So it is done. And this is how it ends.

A quick wave from the gate, and I descend the hill, dead, or at least dying. An hour later, aboard the bus for New York, I drift to sleep. Strange thing: while my eyes are already closed, I hear a voice that sounds like the GF, the old GF, ass-pinching and bombed, saying: Take a breath. Think about this: not long ago, you weren't even here. Thanks to a moment between your mom and dad, a few cells came together, kept multiplying, becoming ears and feet and eyes. Slowly, but not that slowly. Think of it. Gradually, and not very long ago, they became you. And, in a little while, not very long from now, you won't be here, again. But as long as you are, what are you going to do about it?

I open my eyes on a moose, framed by two pines, staring at the bus. Above us hangs a daylight moon like a pale clock-face on the wall of the cosmos. The scale of things suddenly zooms out beyond my wildest imaginings. No one can pretend to understand the sky but I swear I hear it speak. Not to worry, it says. In the scheme of things, all will be well, not to worry, ever, no, no matter what. A perfect blue sky.

Which is how it always looks, before falling.

I'll Love You Always

Agnes Smedley, Writer and Journalist, 1892-1950

I'll Love You Always

Agnes had mega-balls and Angelinalips. Born in Osgood, Missouri to a dirt poor farming clan. Father part Native American. I myself have never met a Native American, though I've seen many on television. Not many. In fact, very few. Almost never. How come? It's their country we stole, isn't it? And TV is hardly the same as life—though with HD and 3-D, some say it's better. Nevertheless, I feel guilty. Maybe when I'm old enough I'll drive to Foxwoods, which is run by the Wampanoags.

Agnes too never finished her formal education yet she was offered a teaching gig anyway. The pattern is now clear: I will never return to school.

* * *

In the distance, New York rises like the kinetic fantasy of a delusional gamer. As we pass Co-Op City, the bus slows to a crawl, and I recall the *Vocals* of old. Our conversations flood in. How we talked about everything. Nothing was off limits: parents, teachers, fapping, the Mayan Calendar, Whitey Vulgar and the Wicked Pissahs, Dragon Age, Goku Fella, and how Barney Frank would look good with a moustache. We mulled suicide, the Decembrists, WikiLeaks, and the Blimp. We wondered aloud if William Shatner was transgendered. We were passionate and beautiful. A minute ago we were in the studio, now I'm a fugitive from my own life. I want to call Rene and explain what just happened with Beyah but no cell, no tell. Do I feel guilty? Nothing happened, yet I do: I feel guilty. The idea of the *Vocals* breaking up kills me because without them, what's left? My family? And what if Serafina never returned? The GF may be starving. I press my face against the glass and stare into the troubled lanes ahead.

* * *

What need for heaven *or* hell when you've got the Bronx? Here every part of a car has an industry devoted to its maintenance and support. I'm sure there's a store that sells only windshield wipers, one for upholstery buttons, door-handles, gloveboxes, grommets. Grommets! Maybe because I've hardly slept, plus I just got the brush-off from the love of my life, I look at the people and the buildings and feel like shouting. Luckily the bus is half empty or I might do some damage—not that I've ever punched so much as a clock. All I know about work, outside of school, is that, somehow, miraculously, it gets done. I mean, the house gets clean no thanks to Mom. My room alone remains off limits, for too many reasons to list. Dad works. Mom worked before she got sick. It's not like I don't know about Astro's life, or Beyah's. They worry about money, fathers in jail, and getting by. My concerns aren't worth a fart to them, I know—and I want to help, but how? Should I move into the projects, maybe?

I miss my iPod like family. More.

Stopped at a light, I think I see Heather the Hot talking with the Suit—that dude I met on GF's roof—like they're friends, which freaks me out until I realize it isn't them.

First sign of trouble: the spastic lights of a cop car double-parked outside Henry's building.

"Where's Ivan?" I ask the uniformed stranger at the door.

"Who?" His round, bearded face suggests a pissed-off Santa. Red-rimmed eyes glare like I just pinched his mother.

"The doorman."

"I'm the doorman. Ivan's gone," he grunts. "I was on vacation. Who the hell are you?"

I explain about my godfather. The not-Ivan tells me the GF was taken to the hospital last night. He nods toward the cop car. "They're looking for you."

My bad day's getting worse with every step. On my way up, I panic. I left the GF, drunk, to sleep it off, so I could chase a dream. But what could happen in a day?

Getting off the elevator is my second mistake (getting on, the first). The atmosphere's like wet cement. First thing I see are two cops standing in the living room, talking to each other. They're young, carnivorous, in short-sleeved shirts. One has a belly dripping over his belt; the other's lean, with a long nose and big jaw. Beyond them, sitting awkwardly in the living room, are my parents.

At that moment, my mother's smoky voice focuses me.

"Jonathan! Where have you been? I've been out of my mind."

You're telling me, I think. Mom's wearing a black dress, which she only does when things are serious, and now I'm worried.

"Don't speak in clichés, Madeline," says Dad. "Let the boy breathe." Like *he* ever has. I look at Dad, who has yet to make eye contact. Here I thought the Suit might jump—now I think the jumper in this story might be me. The nightmare of *familiar* voices.

"I told you not to call the police," he says grimly.

The cops stand there while my parents discuss them.

"We're sorry, Officer Espada," Mom finally says, smiling and brushing her palms down her pants. "As you see, the little criminal has found his way home." She gives me the once-over. "And he looks all right, basically." She turns to me: "Are you all right, honey? No, of course not. Never mind, we'll discuss it later." To the cop: "Is there some paperwork I need to fill out?" Without waiting for an answer, she turns to Dad: "Now you can hurry back to Todd."

"Todd happened to be in New York already. It made sense to join him," Dad says.

The cops look at each other, at my family, at me, the instruments: the whole shebang united in the *The Nightmare Symphony.* "You okay, kid?" the shorter one asks.

I nod. "I'm so sorry." It's true. I'm purple with shame, regret, confusion. I'm tempted to add: You don't know the half of it because if you did, you'd arrest them on charges of reckless parenting, criminal self-absorption, and failure to signal completely relevant changes of heart.

Dad's on the edge of the sofa, right fist bouncing in his left palm like a catcher awaiting the next pitch. Mom sits upright in her cube chair, long-necked, imperious and, probably, stoned. If I shut one eye and cross the other, I can see Dad's nose on my face.

After awkward thanks, the cops practically race each other for the elevator.

"Why don't you go too," Mom says to Dad. She shakes

her long black (dyed) hair in a shudder of scorn.

"Madeline, enough."

"Enough? I'll tell you what..." Her wide-set eyes draw back. "You self-involved little bastard..."

"Now we begin! Listen, Maddie..."

I bounce from one to the other. They've forgotten me already. It's because they're still "young." People say fifty-five is the new thirty-five. How this is possible I have no idea, but people do say it. I'd cut my losses and run, but at that moment Serafina walks in with Asia. For a few seconds my little sister's bright face rewires the room.

"I'm so sorry!" Serafina cries, running over to me. Now I'm not sure which way to turn. I'm trapped. Asia waits for me to acknowledge her. Smile. Too little too late. Her own smile fades. Mere minutes and the shit's piling in from all sides.

"You were supposed to check in daily!" says Mom.

I understand why she's unhappy. I know I'm far from perfect. Hell, I may never graduate high school. Maybe I'll be homeless, end up in jail, marry tragically. Couldn't even manage one old man in a wheelchair. Haven't written a hit song. Not a week alone, and my life's a mess.

When she's done outlining my sins—and they are legion, granted, so it takes a while—what's left to say except: "How is he?"

The unhappy couple trade glances. I'm feeling shittier by the minute.

"He's had another stroke," Dad says in that voice he puts on when he thinks he's being manly and not pulling punches.

Super-honest Dad. My know-thyself papa, in tight jeans that highlight his slim ass, and a v-neck black cashmere. Shaved head bent forward, patrician nose aimed at the floor, blunting the confusion of eye contact.

But who am I to talk? I was supposed to stay with the GF. The job description was basic enough. "Shit. Can I see him?"

Mom shoots me a look. I dare her to say "*Watch your language!*"

"We just came from there," Dad says quickly, as though afraid I might insist on a return visit.

"We spent an hour with him," Mom adds. "Stop slouching. And take your hands out of your pockets! Did you know there's a turtle here?"

She looks heartbroken. I won't add to her pain. I'd forgotten about Davis too. Must be starving. Forgot about everybody. "I'm going now," I say, turning. "First I have to feed the turtle."

Mom's voice sweetens: "Honey, he's not in good shape."

"Who, the turtle?"

"Henry. Your godfather," she says sharply.

Good shape, I think: was he in good shape before? My godfather—but what was he to you? I don't ask.

* * *

Circa 1912, Agnes Smedley had an abortion. Consider the relevance. Not long after, Smedley divorced (not because of the abortion, which her husband encouraged) and moved to New

York, where her ex's family helped her get a job as a secretary. She began taking courses but family pressures pursued her. Her brother, driven by the need for cash, was arrested and sent to jail for stealing a horse. Agnes sent him money and was ready to send more when she learned he'd died on a chain gang, digging a sewer ditch.

* * *

"We're just going back to our hotels," Dad says when I return from the kitchen. "I'm staying at the Plaza..."

"With Todd," Mom contributes, looking at me.

"It's Memorial Day. Impossible to find anything. A virus of tourists has infected the city, as I'm sure you've seen," he explains, coughing into his fist as he pushes himself up off the sofa.

I nod. Memorial Day. The traffic. I think back to Memorial Days past: six hours of laughter at the Brattle watching a Marx Brothers marathon; going to Circus Smirkus when Asia was less than a year old and being invited by the clown to ride a unicycle before hundreds; crawling into the parental sloop at daybreak so that Dad could hoist me up on his feet and I could soar like Superman above their bed. More than once such miracles occurred. Are they erased forever by what's happening now?

"I'm at the Hilton," says Mom. "Near the Modern. *I* had no trouble finding a room."

I take a long look at my poor father, face puffed out by antidepressants. His shaved head's mottled, eyes bloodshot. And Mom. Mom. Tiny invisible whips lash her from within. Her rage is aimed at Dad but I suspect it's been there for centuries. I don't know if she wants to murder the bard or fuck him blind. Or maybe she'd rather just shoot us all. It happens. I wish I could help—but I can't, and I know it. Lucky for her, her bone structure alone guarantees that no one will notice until the venom of her dark and paralyzing love has entered their bloodstream. Call me when you grow up, I want to say. But that would be dumb.

They look at each other with a skepticism that, for all I know, may be a kind of love. For a moment we're frozen like we're posed for a family portrait amid the ruins—of instruments that can't be played and skeletons from a past no one will explain, maybe because they don't understand it themselves.

"Why didn't you answer your cell?" Mom asks.

"I lost it," I say.

"Get another. Right away. You still have my card?"

I nod.

"Do it at once. Please. Better yet, take mine. Here. Take it. And call me. Every day. You hear me? Every day." She thrusts it in my direction. I frown into its ugly android face. What apps has she got?

"Where will I call you?"

"At the hotel."

Then Asia runs up and gives me a hug. I clutch her so hard I fear I'll crack those sparrow bones.

"I miss you," she says.

I kiss her forehead, pick up the phone. "Miss you too, Asia." She, at least, looks bereft.

"You go to the hospital with him, Serafina," Mom says in her take-no-prisoners voice.

Serafina's lips cinch.

GF may be one of Dad's best friends but Todd's in town. Like me and Beyah, I guess. When love calls, the sick go begging.

The elevator door opens. To my surprise, Dad adds: "I think you should come home, Jonathan. This is no place to be running around on your own."

Home? I think, but don't say it: and where would that be?

"You told me to stay with GF, Dad. I fucked up. I'm sorry. I'll stay. I want to stay. You also gave me an assignment. I'm working on it. I'll hang here until he gets back and I finish my essay. Okay?"

Dad can't hide his relief. The lines around his jaw relax. He turns from me to Serafina: "Obviously you won't be needed here for the next few days. I'll call you when we know Henry's release date."

* * *

"It's so sad," Serafina says as the elevator door closes. "What happened to *Senhor* Henry. He was getting better."

What's sad is how you treat your own kids, I want to say, but don't. Who am I to point the finger? Besides, she suddenly looks tired. What will she do now that Dad's sending her home?

The elevator stops four times going down. As others board, we fall silent until reaching ground.

"The subway is there," she points across the street.

I flick Mom's credit card back and forth like a flag and wave down a passing cab. Inside, I look out the window but what I see is Beyah by the lake in the light saying *Go*. When we get to the hospital, I swipe the card but it's declined. Blood rushes to my cheeks. Someone hasn't been paying her bills. Or maybe she just cut me off. Or the cab's machine broke. What do they do to you if you can't pay your fare? I turn to Serafina for help. She gives me a look I've not seen from her before. I study my sneakers, which are starting to smell pretty funky. Then she digs into her large blue bag. Strange how one small sweep of a card changes things. I feel unplugged. My energy's gone.

* * *

Approaching the hospital door, Serafina begins to walk slower. She frowns. I've seen the same lines on Beyah. We stand at the corner of 59th and 10th Avenue. Traffic actually seems lighter. An orange sun stains the sidewalk, and I'm sweating again.

"I can't, Jonatan. I can't go in." She stops, forcing people to walk around us.

"Why not?"

"I just can't, child, is all. There's too much sadness in the world. Too much." She pinches the bridge of her nose with two fingers, shakes her head, squeezes her eyes. These Brazilians and I seem to be good at making each other cry. And suddenly I understand all. Why she can't go home or visit her husband; why she lies. Why Dad lied—mainly to himself—all these years. Why he had to stop. I don't understand why Mom pulled out her teeth, but let it go. Too much sadness all around. People do what they can to hide from it. When one thing stops working, they look for new ways. But that only makes things worse. Serafina pulls me to herself like a pillow. I breathe deeper. And, while a bus blasts past, and ambulances wail, my nose burrows in red silk, my arms circle her waist, and we hug, silencing for a moment all the sadness and tears in the universe. Undreamed. Unhappened. Nothing ever was but us, holding each other, only my face between her breasts, sipping a cocktail of lemons and cheese.

And then….

Boing!

Serafina jerks away, her face a mockery of shock. Leans back, squints. Laughs and musses my hair roughly. "Bad boy!" Her tongue slips in and out between her teeth. Throws her head back and laughs so hard there's spit flying and I see two gold caps at the back of her mouth. I think maybe she's gonna hug me again, that this has places to go. Lolita the Update. Alas. She leans over, pecks me on the cheek and, grinning, says: "I'll tell Beyah you're looking for her."

"Thanks," I say, wiping my eyes.

* * *

I stand outside the hospital door, counting the number of people who enter wearing red sneakers. Not that many. Country's dying from dwarfism of the imagination, Henry once said.

In the torrent of a city street, cars and people whiz by with so much purpose you want to stop and quiz each one to find out where they're going, where they've been, and if it's worth the trip, because maybe they know something you don't. Soon you're holding your breath while forgetting even your name, because surely what you have to do isn't half as necessary as the missions of the frenzied hoards. In a panic, I call Rene.

"Oh, it's you," she says. "Thanks for thinking of me," she continues. "Really, I'm touched by your concern."

She goes on this way a bit, and I don't blame her. I suck on the bars of her gripe. Meanwhile, across the street, kids in black spandex race by. Each carries someone larger than himself on his back. Then I see their trainer jogging in a bright red jacket that says *West Side Alpine Club*. For a moment I'm tempted to join them.

"I lost my phone," I say.

"So whose is this? Your mom's?"

I explain some of what happened—omitting the bit about Beyah.

"And you don't know how he is?"

"I'm about to find out," I say. I can feel her holding back. She knows what I want—for her to tell me it's okay, that I didn't do anything wrong, that everything will work out. Should have known better than to call Rene. She's a positive person and all, and I'm crazy about her, but she knows in her bones that not everything works out. As it did not, for the parents who gave her away; as it did, for the ones who took her in; as it may, or may not, for her. Or for us.

"We've got a lot to talk about," she says. "When you coming home?"

"What? I'm losing you. Damn." I put the phone back in my pocket. My lowest point.

Finally I enter St. Luke's. The hospital has the breathless, frenzied feel of an airport, people rushing by, announcements over the PA, phones sounding everywhere. I walk toward the information desk, growing smaller and more frightened with each step.

GF's alone when I enter. The white room hums. TV's tuned to a talk show. A group of people sit around a table, discussing the economy. Strips of numbers scroll across the bottom of the screen like subtitles in a foreign film in which every word of dialogue means *money*. Not the kind of thing he ever watched. This is what happens when strangers take over your life.

At first he looks fine. Eyes half shut. Only, I can't tell whether he's asleep or awake. And then I realize that, most likely, neither can he.

Outside, the ceaseless murmur of nurses and the noisy gossip of health are unable to mask completely the low-voltage hum of sickness and dying. Does anyone feel better in a hospital? I'd sooner rot in a cave than under the glare of lights that never quite go out. But who's asking?

His hair's neatly combed. I again admire how thick and

dark it is, but for the strip of white running down the middle like a dividing line on a highway. His tongue pushes past his lips. His breath comes hard and slow and from way far away. His eyes look open, but when I say "Hey," there's hardly a flicker.

What's happened to all the people he met along the way? Those ladies I saw him with? Mom sure didn't look eager to hang out with him. Seems like a man goes out of circulation more quickly than a magazine.

A flip-book from the years I've known him: GF beside me in the dinosaur room at the Museum of Natural History, pointing out that T-Rex didn't have a penis, only a cloacal sac, imagine; on ice with Asia and Mom at Rockefeller Plaza the year Dad decides he needs to be at a writer's retreat over Christmas. Then there's the night two years ago at the party for Dad's latest shattering volume when the GF decides I need a driving lesson. We're both looped. Nevertheless he urges me behind the wheel of his Audi for a spin down Memorial Drive. I shift like the devil until we return to the driveway where, mistaking the clutch for the brake, I ram Dad's baby-blue Miata.

He was the king of Good Times, was GF—and he was more, the guy I went to when I needed someone there. Until this trip. He'll be a lot to miss. He was my ally, the one adult I trusted and sort-of counted on. Now tubes up his nose help him breathe, and dinner's the pin in his arm. Little electronic noises ping around us like an early video game.

It occurs to me I might never see him again as he was. This sets me thinking about people I used to know but no longer do: Debbie from second grade, whose family moved to Boulder. I guess there's a chance I'll run into her, but not likely. My third-grade buddy Glen, who last year flew his skateboard off the Zakim Bridge and sailed into the firmament of glory in our hood. My grandfather and grandmother on Mom's side. They'd made a pact. When she passed, he put a bullet in his heart. It did the trick.

Quick exits. I like it. Like it fine. GF is different. He loves being here. Definitely.

The phone rings. I'm guessing Mom, and switch to vibrate.

Can a man shrink to half his size in one day? His parted lips appear to move, but no sounds come. He may never say another word. I might never have the answers to my questions. I won't even know what I don't know.

What exactly do I want to say to him? Everything's moving so fast and I got a feeling nothing's slowing down any time soon. His tongue wiggles like it's the last part of him that's still alive. Death. That's what he's looking at on some invisible screen behind his eyes; it's what I see in him. It's taking him the way he was made, cell by cell.

Down the hall, someone screams. A nurse pops her head in: "Everything OK in here?" I shrug. *Sure, jolly. Just a nice quiet little death in progress. Nothing more. A private affair. I'm sure you have plenty of other deaths to check in on.* She looks from me to the GF, then retreats.

I think to myself: what if this was me? What if these were my last days on the planet? What would I want to do? Who would I want to see? Maybe no one. Would I pray? If so, I'd have to teach myself to do it. What's amazing is that I don't have answers to these questions yet what could matter more? Everybody gets here, eventually.

I imagine saying my last goodbye to Rene. We're on a mountain top, where a wind whips the high grasses and bulging clouds behind which the orange sun slowly sinks, and her soft lips tremble. A lone nightingale in a tree raises its throat in song. Mine is another voyage, I say to her, licking her tears with my too tainted tongue.

I begin again: "Something else. You may not know it but you helped me out a lot. You showed me things Dad never could. You taught me how to drive. Remember the time you took me to see the dinosaurs? Listen, I'm glad you and Mom had a thing. Maybe you and Dad did too. It's cool. All cool. Without you, I wouldn't be here. (Strictly speaking, it's the truest thing I've said.) Sorry. I feel stupid talking like this. I have no idea if this makes any sense or if you even hear me. But thanks anyway, GF. Really, thanks."

I put my hand on his forehead. A gurgle bubbles from his throat. Is he dying? Did I help kill him? My feet sink into the floor. I lean forward, close to his ear, until I can smell the old skin and alcohol. His eyes dart under the lids.

"See ya, GF."

I straighten, pull my chin down to my chest and raise a fist in the air: "Fight the power." But my voice has no fight left in it.

* * *

On my way out, I pass through a large common room. The walls are beige, the floor gleams like it was polished with high-gloss piss. Walking, I squeak.

A silver-haired, baby-faced crooner stands before a captive audience of fifty or so mainly old ladies in chairs and hospital beds. More than half are asleep. The ones who aren't would as soon stone as hear him. The fluorescent lights turn everything milky-pale. A woman laid out on a padded electric bed zips by, emitting bat-squeaks. Desperate, the singer begs his audience to clap in rhythm. One nurse tries, and gets the beat. The others either stare or snore. Segueing into *I'll Love You Always*, the singer invites his audience to dance. It's like he's deaf and blind himself. Who does he think he's playing to? An old man with dirty gray hair down to his shoulders hobbles to the front and starts waltzing. Alone. His arms embrace the air. His johnny falls open, flashing his thin ass. Then a big-boned woman, who until now appeared to be dozing, seizes the moment. Rises. She's not wearing a hospital gown—she's not even a patient. She grabs the old fart's hands, which are smaller than hers, and they begin shuffling together to no music we hear, like they're dancing to please God. Why else would you bother?

* * *

In China Smedley organized a square dance attended by Mao, who, as you might expect, had two left feet. When she told him so, Mao's wife slapped her. So Smedley, she hit her right back.

Let me say right here that I've fallen in love with Agnes Smedley. You would too, if you knew her better. It's her nerve. She told the bastards who tried pushing her around to go fuck themselves. Smedley backed away from no one: not Mao, or Stalin, not even Joe McCarthy scared her. And, in the end, it was her own people who got her, of course.

When she was older, Smedley lived at Yaddo, a writer's colony Dad occasionally stays at in upstate New York. There she was accused of spying because she'd published books supporting the Chinese Communist Revolution. Again with the commies! The poet Robert Lowell led the charge to fire the woman who ran Yaddo for giving Smedley space. Here's where it gets personal. Dad knew this Lowell dude. He took his "famous" workshop at Harvard, which he flunked. How you flunk poetry-writing I don't know. Nevertheless, Dad worshipped the man. Not only had they gone to the same snooty schools, their parents socialized together. Dad used to recite this poem called "Skunk Hour" like it was the 23rd Psalm. The only line I remember from it is "My mind's not right."

Amen.

Exiled from Yaddo, Agnes Smedley left America and moved to England, where she died, pretty much broke, from complications after surgery for an ulcer. You'll find her ashes in the Baboashan Revolutionary Cemetery in Beijing.

* * *

Screaming sirens wake me. I stumble to the window. There's urgency in the air, like someone's been calling my name for hours and I'm just tuning in. I see cop cars, an ambulance, and a crowd fanned out around the sidewalk below my window. Right away, I know what's happened.

I struggle into pants and slap my face with water from the kitchen sink. The elevator takes a long time to arrive. There are people in the lobby, a brush-fire of whispers. Outside, the doorman's bending over something spread out on the sidewalk, and I know it's him. The guy from the roof I met my first night here. The Suit.

The yellow tape of crime scenes keeps me back but I can see, through the tangle of emergency legs, an out-stretched arm. And in that arm—in a fist at the end of the arm—I see the flesh-toned torso of a headless doll. Although she's headless, I hear her bleating *Help me! Help me!*

I turn away. I scan the faces of the crowd: another bad night on the town, one more dream deferred, and then it's time for work, or play, or whatever else the grown-ups do inside their so-called lives. *Help me* cries the doll.

I look up toward the roof: the building seems to touch the sky, whose blue again seems clueless as the mind of God. The doorman's talking to the cops while Mrs. McCloskey sobs into her fist. Several dozen strangers scan the sidewalk for a key to what their morning rounds have led them to: a rain of men, forecasting what?

I wake up in a sweat.

* * *

Mom called the landline many times today. At least I think it's her. I've got the answering machine off. Curled in bed, staring out the window at the world below. I have thought, seriously and with mounting excitement, about jumping off the roof myself. If I screamed from the top, would anybody hear me? Eventually I settle into the silence: an exhausting, stupid quiet. A silence all about *me*, how fucked my life is.

Day turns to night, so some things never change. I read myself to sleep.

* * *

In the cab to the hospital I'd asked Serafina where she sometimes disappeared to. She got very quiet and looked out the window. In her profile, I saw Beyah. I had to bite my lip to keep from crying out: I crazy love your daughter! As it was I must have groaned or something because she looked over at me. She leaned toward me, took my hand in hers, and said: "Jonatan, I cannot tell you everything." Then she went on to say that she had lied about her family being in Brazil— obviously, as I knew. She said her husband was in prison, and that she was working with a lawyer who did immigration stuff. Before his stroke, the GF had been helping her. I didn't ask how she met him. Anyway, that's where she snuck off to when she could. She was trying to get her husband out. Why didn't she visit her family in Jersey more often, I wondered but didn't have the chance to ask. Then she made me promise not to say a word. "Who will hire me if they know my man's locked up?" I had hardly any time to take this in because the cab pulled up in front of the hospital and I proceeded to be financially embarrassed.

* * *

All week I've tried not thinking what I can't stop thinking about. I report now that it hasn't worked. Sometimes I imagine watching Rene swell day by day until one night a tiny Smedley pops, rising out of her like a Brazilian fire balloon. It tears across the sky, redefining the night: another me (plus her, of course) on earth. And I think Oh Fuck, where will the child live? Who will teach it to crawl? Never mind college tuition. And then I think of what it might be like to close the chapter fast. Slam it shut. Laminate it. Seal it off for good, and move on. Could we pull that off? Never mind. This one is her call. In the end, we'll do whatever Rene wants. I think we'll wind up in Baja California, where we'll live beside the whales, learn their language, and absorb their lore. The lives we'd lead if we could learn from whales!

* * *

This is the graph where I tell you what I've learned, how I've reconciled with my parents and all. But that would be bull. I may never know what went down between them and the

GF—something big, I guess. And who would it help if I did know, if suddenly their past made sense, and all became as clear as Sunday? Did chasing Beyah make sense? Do the lives of the writers I've "studied" make sense?

Some things have worked out. I know where I belong. I know who my friends are. And that's not a bad place to start. We can do it. We can make this whole thing swing the other way. I have a plan. It involves Rene, and the Virgins, and you. If, together, we resist the pricks who think they have the right to make us small and our lives nothing, who will stop us, and what way?

* * *

And then I listened to my messages.

The Great Crimes of the Future

The Great Crimes of the Future

The air that day was stroke-inducing, yet the church was full. An early hot spell had settled over the region, the building's central air was on the fritz, and the place smelled like rotten carp. Thunderstorms were predicted but the morning sun was brutal. Also, it was a Tuesday, which has always seemed to me the saddest day of the week.

As I was filing in, a woman in a pew toward the back grabbed my forearm. She folded toward me. Her sharply angled face was lean yet full of creases and her eyes blazed. Her warm breath was damp. "She was a wonderful woman," the stranger said. I nodded, pulling away. Who were all these people who suddenly had a claim on me? I felt their stares as I walked to front of the church.

I'd no idea she knew so many, who'd care enough to say goodbye. They were all colors, sizes, styles: black and brown, natty and ragged. Some looked homeless; one arrived in a chauffeured Hummer. A few I recognized, but most were strangers. The open space filled with whispers which seemed to float above me in a cloud of voices, fluttering like moths. Somewhere in the back, off and on, displaying perfect timing, a baby wailed.

I sat between Rene and Asia, who sobbed throughout the service. I held her tight, but couldn't calm her. Her sparrow

211

bones felt tinier than ever. Nothing settled her for weeks, and I'll forever worry how she deals with this over time.

Rene cast up her chin and squeezed my arm. Did people think that that was where the sadness lived?

I felt nothing. My eyes kept going to the windows. Tall and peaked, they let in light which never seemed to reach me, like it stopped just at the threshold of where I began (but I'd begun in her), hitting up against a shield of darkness through which I saw and yet couldn't believe what I was seeing, what was happening around me. My mother, yesterday so vital and so crazy, was dead. I repeated the word over and over. It meant nothing, a foreign word for which there was no accurate translation.

My father, sitting next to Asia, sheathed in black, sighed loudly. He looked angry, as though yet again my mother had affronted him, this time by dying. I could hardly stand to see him.

The Unitarian minister, whom I'd met before, and who'd always seemed too bright and chatty, praised her volunteer work. He called her charismatic, describing how he'd met her in the women's prison. He told us how she brought the women books and gave them hope, and stuff like that. I heard his words but couldn't take them in. Later, I wished I'd recorded them. But I was wearing a suit and tie for like the third time in my life, and all I could think about was how wet and itchy my white shirt was.

* * *

When the phone rang in my godfather's apartment that morning a few days earlier, I assumed it was Mom and ignored it.

Around noon, I finally got out of bed. I foraged in the fridge for breakfast, which I devoured sitting out on the deck, watching people snaking in and out of Central Park. While flipping through what I'd done of my assignment, I thought about our joy ride to Atlantic City, and my equally insane pursuit of Beyah, and realized I'd never finish.

Near the end of the day, I checked Mom's cell. There were eighteen messages plus texts, each telling me to call home at once.

I phoned Rene, who said to call Dad but wouldn't say why. By the sound of her voice, I knew it was bad. From Dad I learned that, early morning of the day before, while I was sleeping under stars upstate, my mother had been found by a cleaning woman in her hotel room. She'd swallowed a bottle of pills: something like thirty Ambien. Did the trick. While he spoke, I stared at the painted square, noticing for the first time how what seemed blue from a distance contained traces of red and purple and orange. There's so much we never see, even when we look right at a thing.

I thought about the writers I'd discovered, how hard *their* lives had been. Agnes Smedley kept coming to mind. Her mother beat her. Her grandmother mocked her. She was a sensitive child, forced to fend for herself from the start. She watched her brother killing himself with booze. She saw the system that betrayed them. And she decided to fight back. Her looks, as well as her chutzpah, reminded me of Mom. All the writers had to deal with whatever world they woke in. They had two choices: speak up, or play dead. They refused to take life lying down, said slavery was fucked, that women had rights, and the poor, and gay people—even Dad! Each found a voice that rose above the crap they feed us every day. A voice that said *I bet the folks we're screwing now have rights we haven't thought of yet, and by the "way" what are their names? Now that we've killed them, isn't it polite to ask?*

They stuck up for whoever needed them. In finding the right words for their lives, they sprang themselves, and us, maybe not totally free, but closer.

The things they don't teach you in school would fill a book.

At the cemetery, I drifted away from the crowd at the grave until I suddenly found myself in a quiet place, out of sight of the rest. I sat down under a willow. There was a small hole in the ground near my feet. Where did it lead, I wondered. What lived there? Death, I thought, was like this hole. No, it was a doorway in the very air itself, into which people slipped while you weren't looking. Turn away for a minute, and you never know who might be gone when you look back. Maybe that's why people tell you never to look back. But is that really possible? I stared at the ground for a long time before getting up and rejoining the others.

* * *

The next few months were tough. After the abortion, Rene fell into a depression. Though she appeared to bounce back pretty quickly, she seemed a little less glad to know me. That fall, her parents transferred her to a private school on the other side of town. We stayed in touch until she left for college in California. I told her I still hoped to meet the whales of Baja, but by then we both knew that was that, and so it was.

After extremes, I sought the middle: Ohio is where I went to school, and where, for now, I live.

* * *

Our century was founded on three crimes. As every child can name them, I won't belabor what we can't undo. I can account only for mine. Of course I echoed what the world around me had got into. But I'd atoned, and had been forgiven. Nearly a decade out, Astro and I remain the best of friends.

To the amazement of all, my godfather got better. While he never recovered full use of his legs, he was eventually able to get back into the courtroom. We speak by phone a couple of times a year. He told me he succeeded in getting Serafina's husband out of jail, and eventually secured a visa for him. I hear Mirabai is married, with a child of her own. And I saw on Facebook that Rene is starting on her PhD in Marine Biology at the University of Texas in Austin next year.

In time, I learned it's possible to love the dead, and be loved back by them in turn. About a year ago, my mother began showing up. She appeared as a kind of higher awareness, a presence somewhere in my brain, without a body or even an image, yet distinct enough for me to talk to. I told her I was sorry; I described my work at school, and asked her what she thought of the several girls who'd moved in and out of my life before I finally met Alba. Though I've never heard Mom answer, I always intuit a response, and that's plenty.

I write this sitting in our studio apartment. Alba's in the next room, finishing her applications to med school. I'm working at the local cable station, learning about cameras, gaffers, and Bozo boxes. I'm also making my first film, about a tree. There's an apple tree outside our small building. It's really old and part of it was blown down in a storm last March. But the branch that broke off wasn't completely severed from the trunk. Even lying, broken, on the ground, the tree continues to bear fruit. The best apples come from there. I'm not sure why I think there's a story here, but I do.

My father has grown a beard so big and white, I call it Moby Dick. He and I now speak by phone several times a month. He wants Alba and me to join him and Todd for Thanksgiving this year, and we're inclining yes. I still hate holidays, but sometimes, what else can you do?

Acknowledgments

This short novel has been long on friends encountered along the way. My thanks to: Lara Stecewycz, Thaila Ramanujan, Erica Mena, Catherine Parnell, John Fulton, Martha Cooley, Susan Cheever, Tom Sleigh, George Scialabba, Tom Bahr, William Hayes, Charles Capro, Larry Lee, Jae Mae Barizo, Bill Pierce, Erin Gilbert, Julie Batten, Warren Hinckle and, of course, Laura Scholz, aka "Ms. Precious Little."

For decades I've wanted to shout out thanks to my twelfth grade English teacher at Cramford High School, Barbara Buettner, for her early encouragement. Without it, I doubt *Smedley* would be here today.

Merci bien to Pietre Valbuena for his marvelous cover art.

And, for sure, to Peter Sarno for believing in old Smedley.

Finally, I've said it before, and I'll say it again: Thanks, Alex

Reading Group Guide

1. How is Jonathan's "assignment" more of an opportunity than a punishment?

2. Can you imagine a time when pursuing reading and writing might feel subversive, a kind of rebellion, a kind of freedom? Is it possible that recent technologies might lure more readers to engage with literature?

3. Is Jonathan too tough on his father? Most of us remember things our parents said or did which we thought at the time—perhaps correctly—were unjust. Have you ever changed your mind about how you reacted then? Can you imagine responding differently?

4. How would you react if you were to find yourself in Jonathan's situation?

5. What advice would you give to Rene and Jonathan?

6. What choice did Jonathan's father have? How else might he have behaved?

7. What do you make of Jonathan's "crime"? Have you ever done something out of peer pressure, in reaction to social forces, or a particular climate of opinion? Can you imagine how you might stop yourself from doing so again? Are we ever completely free of external influences? How do we overcome social conditioning which doesn't correspond to our values?

8. What do you make of Jonathan's biographical sketches of once-famous, now forgotten writers?

9. Make your own list of books or writers everyone should know, for different reasons.

10. Do you ever find yourself more interested a writer's biography than in his or her work? Have you ever learned something about a writer which made you reevaluate a book you loved? What changed your mind? Should a writer's biography affect how we read their work?

11. Late in the novel, Jonathan declares "The things they don't teach you in school would fill a book." So many of the writer's Jonathan selects were autodidacts. Does school prepare us for life beyond its walls? What would you propose as an ideal curriculum?

12. Jonathan wonders how he might show his solidarity with some of his more besieged friends. Should he feel guilty for being born into a world of privilege? Why? Or, why not?

13. What special significance or associations does the name "Smedley" have for Jonathan?

AUTHOR QUESTIONS:

This book is so different from your first three novels.

I see each book as an experiment. It begins in a need, an impulse, an itch that's more physical than mental—a kind of pressure lodged somewhere in my body which the act of writing alone is able to relieve. Anyway, I never know what voice is going to whisper in my ear, or why, or what it wants. My task, at least initially, when starting a book is to attend, to be present, to record as much as it's willing to give. Some days it's generous, others nearly mute. The "bad" days (and they're not always actually "bad") are when my conscious mind kicks in and I start thinking about structure, and start the nearly endless process of tinkering with sentences.

Where did the idea for this come from?

Jonathan's voice first arose just as I was entering the heavy-lifting phase of eldercare with my parents. It helped me through many a rough day in the nursing homes, hospitals, and rehab centers which have become such a regular part of my routine.

I remember feeling kind of overwhelmed, sitting in the Cambridge Public Library, flipping through Aubrey's *Brief Lives*. It's a series of short, gossipy biographical sketches, written in the 17th century, about various acquaintances and contemporaries of Aubrey's, including people like Milton and the poet Lovelace. While reading, I "heard" a voice making all kinds of wisecracks, prying between the lines of what Aubrey wrote and what he actually meant to communicate. The voice made me laugh, something I really needed at the time.

Once I had tuned into that voice, I kept wanting to know what it might say about X or Y....It was the narrator's sassiness that appealed to me. His shoot-from-the-hip attitude helped keep up my spirits while surrounded by the responsibilities and inevitable sadnesses associated with the aging of loved ones.

As I was writing, the Occupy Movement was unfolding here, with many echoes around the world. A new generation of young people was beginning to take part in the remaking of our planet—a thing our earth sorely needs. I was thrilled. Jonathan, though far from the front lines, became a spiritual fellow-traveler with his peers worldwide. That's why the book is dedicated "to the rebel soul in everyone."

What are some of the challenges that come with writing from the POV of a fifteen year old?

He's not just any fifteen year old! He's a scion of privilege, who has grown up in one of the most exclusive and elitist enclaves in the world. His father is a WASP; his mother is a secular Jew. In short, he's a lot farther from me than many readers will understand. In many ways, he's farther from me than Mme X, a middle-aged British Jew who lived through the London blitz, whose voice I assumed in my last novel, *The House of Widows.*

If Jonathan's world was completely foreign to me, his hometown of Cambridge, where I arrived in 1976, was once a good place in which to be poor. I used to bounce checks regularly at the Evergood Market, which I learned recently is owned by the family of Peter Segal, who does that show *Wait Wait Don't Tell Me* on the radio. I'd walk in and find my check tacked to a bulletin board next to the cash register for all to see. Yet the owners always let me redeem it, and continued taking checks from me even though—and I'm not exaggerating—for a time, every other one bounced....

So, for me to write in the voice of a child who'd grown up inside all this privilege was in a way my attempt to find out if I had put my prejudices behind me. Could I see the world through his eyes? Could I empathize with him, despite his privileges? Whether or not I've succeeded is of course for readers to decide for themselves.

For all that, in a funny way this feels like my most personal book. Aside from my delight at inhabiting the skin of the randy fifteen year old, there were things I felt able to say...or that I heard myself saying, which I'd never imagined getting into. It helps that Jonathan's a rebel, and not a snob.

When his professor-father tells him to write a history of literature in the age of Twitter, Smedley responds by focusing on a quite unusual list of writers.

I've heard that some people have been puzzled by the writers Jonathan picks for his essay. Certainly they're not the usual suspects. It would have been easy, and tempting, as well as perhaps more commercially savvy, to pick the familiar and the enshrined: Woolf, Borges, Calvino, Sebald, etc. These are the "cool" international writers properly beloved by readers. But they are just part of the story. There are many others equally worthy of our attention.

You might call part of the book's secret project both an attempt at rethinking our received ideas about the classics, as well as a bit of fun had with the whole notion of a conclusive list of "the great books." The hierarchies which haunt so many aspects of our contemporary civilization, always expressed in numerical terms—top ten lists, our fifty richest people, our hundred best restaurants, etc—are rarely, if ever, definitive.

But the list is far from arbitrary—and was, in earlier drafts, a lot longer. In fact, most of the writers Jonathan selects were rebels of one sort or another, from the 17th century courtier Richard Lovelace, who wrote what's perhaps the greatest prison poem in the language ("Stone walls do not a prison make...) to Agnes Smedly, born dirt-poor in poor in Osgood, Missouri, to a coal-miner father, who began her career as a school teacher in rural Colorado and wound up as an international correspondent writing for papers in Germany, France, China, India and the US. She fell in love with an Indian spy, taught Mao to dance, lived for years at Yaddo, a writer's colony in upstate New York, but died broke in London, and is buried in Beijing. I think of her as a kind of early version of Amy Goodman/Terry Gross hybridized with Martha Gellhorn.

Like most kids his age, Jonathan is totally immersed in the virtual world.

Yes, he spends a lot of his time online. But in the last part of the book, he leaves his iPad at home, and then he loses his cell phone. When he finally faces Beyah, who he believes is the object of his desire, he's essentially naked. It's just one human being facing another—no texting, no screens.

Though he's grown up in a world of icons and endless visual stimulation, he gradually discovers the singular power of presence, print, and, even, inwardness.

Despite Jonathan's protestations, this does indeed seem like a coming of age story.

Yes and no. I kind of agree with Jonathan when he says that no one comes of age anymore. Okay, most people do settle on a self and stick with it. At the same time, we are porous beings and invaders are boring into us from all sides. Despite our privileges and first-world advantages—or because of them—we're incredibly vulnerable to the temptations of consumerism, among other things.

At the same time, I have high hopes that Jonathan, having felt the consequences of his family's instability, will move through life a little more aware of the ways in which our actions ripple out and affect others.

Given the liberal atmosphere in which Jonathan was raised, I was taken aback by the "racial" aspect of his "crime."

I was too. The incident "happened" without my planning it, and when it did, I was sufficiently disturbed to want to change the "victim" from Astro to Klyt but in the end I let it stand because I wanted to suggest that even among the most enlightened and privileged there are moments and areas of moral blindness. And while most of the conversation these days is about Michael Brown and Eric Garner, I remind myself that the first high-profile incident highlighting our embedded racism took place right here in Cambridge, Massachusetts, when a policeman arrested the great African American scholar Henry Louis Gates for entering his own home—which happens to be in a tony and otherwise largely homogeneous neighbor-hood.

The book does seem like more than just a straight-forward narrative about a rebellious teenager. There is, for example, that short theory of fiction in the middle.

You're referring to that excerpt ostensibly written by Jonathan's father. I wanted this book to work on several levels. On the one hand it is what it appears to be: the story of a kid growing up in a family that's falling apart. It's happening during a period rich in contrasts. We have, today, a heightened awareness of racial and economic disparities, and that seems "healthy." On the other hand, the disparities not only exist—they continue to grow. The discontents of civilization appear to balance out its benefits. We have gay marriage and we have Trayvon Martin. Technology is allowing us to expand the possibilities for the most vulnerable among us—the mentally and physically disabled—while the damage done by our foreign and environmental policies have resulted in the decimation of a part of the world my eighth grade history teacher called "the cradle of civilization."

Anyway, the structure seemed to invite me to do several things at once. I could include a "theory" of fiction and reading because it made sense in the context of Jonathan's project.

And, of course, it's also a story about the malleability of identity. I remember a poet—I think it was Robert Bly—muttering one evening: "Identity is so fragile." That's a striking notion, isn't it? I mean, we present ourselves very clearly as *Janet* or *Carl*....but the whole picture isn't quite so obvious.

You've taught Creative Writing for a long time. What's the relationship between your teaching and your creative work? Does it hurt, or in any way affect, your work as a writer?

Everyone needs a day job. Even monks; even the rich, who are, after all, just poor people with money. From any day job you can extrapolate a lot about what it means to work in America.

Teaching can be profoundly creative, and important. According to Buddha, teaching was a lot more valuable than the performing of miracles. Effective teaching, thanks to which another being is able to move forward in her life, is itself transformative and therefore miraculous (because all miracles are essentially transformations). I thank my high school English teacher, Barbara Buettner, daily for putting me on the path....

On the other hand, I never wanted or expected to teach. That I've done so, for over thirty years, and that I still love it, still surprises me.

People say this is the great age of television

....episodes of *The Wire* were indeed Shakespearean. Lena Dunham's *Girls* should inspire all writers of fiction: the boundaries have been pushed pretty far. There's nothing that can't be said, and there's no more teeheeing at images of a biggish girl sporting in the garden of earthly delights. *Wolf Hall*, already a great novel, also made for sublime television.

At the same time, television is television. It is a different medium and the effect of watching it is radically different from the way I feel during, and after, reading. Images on a screen convey one sort of information. It can be rich and nuanced, or it can be witless and silly. But my immersion in language that's been shaped by an artist leaves me in a very different place. I love the way I feel after reading a good sentence or a beautiful line of poetry—it's one of the deepest pleasures I know.

About the Author

Askold Melnyczuk's first novel, *What Is Told*, was a *New York Times Notable Book;* his second, *The Ambassador of the Dead*, was selected as one of the *Best Books of the Year* by the *Los Angeles Times;* the most recent, *The House of Widows*, was chosen by the American Libraries Association's *Booklist* as an Editor's Choice.

He has published stories, poems, essays, translations, and reviews in *The New York Times, The Nation, APR, The Antioch Review, Poetry,* and *Glimmer Train*. Melnyczuk has received numerous awards for his fiction, as well as for his editorial work as founding editor of *Agni* and Arrowsmith Press. He teaches at the University of Massachusetts Boston and in the Bennington Writing Seminars.

Other Books by Askold Melnyczuk

What Is Told

"A marvelous novel and proof once again that the novel is not dead wherever it has work—meaningful work—to do."
Chinua Achebe

"A beautiful book....I just read it and read it and read it and there I was—alone."
Grace Paley

"A great novel of unresentful sorrow and half-requited loss."
Seamus Heaney

"Every so often a novel surpasses all expectations and fills us with the freshness of origins....Askold Melnyczuk is a startlingly inventive stylist—he gets the eyes gulping and the finger tips fidgeting at the edge of the page."
Sven Birkerts

"Magnificent in scope....Brilliantly Melnyczuk skips across decades and continents...His blend of myth and realism, punctuated with violence and comedy recalls Garcia Marquez."
Philip Patrick, *The Boston Globe*

"To fall in love with Melnyczuk's voice is no trouble at all."
Alida Becker, *The New York Times Book Review*

Ambassador of the Dead

"A triumph of style and storytelling....Melnyczuk has brought the great tradition of Russian literature to American soil in a transplant that is a work of art."
Scott Morris, *The LA Times*

"Artistic gold....Melnyczuk is an able analyst of character and a superb storyteller."
Dan Cryer, *Newsday*

"Here's another American Immigration Story, an exquisite, original one..."
Carolyn See, *The Washington Post*

"A very powerful and disturbing novel...Melnyczuk explores profound questions related to violence, the weight of the past, and the kind of pain from which it is impossible to recover."
Library Journal

"Melnyczuk doesn't shrink from the difficulties raised by Ukrainian history...This is beautiful stuff."
Jeffrey Eugenides, *The New York Times Book Review*

"Luminous and haunting."
Publisher's Weekly

"Fresh and stunning."
Barry Hannah

"A novel so precise and understated it's stunning."
Esquire

House of Widows

"A dazzling novel."
Howard Zinn

"Irresistable."
Jumpha Lahiri

"A big novel…about love, war, duty, honor, betrayal, history, and
politics. Hard to put down and harder to forget."
Booklist

"Melnyczuk's hallucinatory tale achieves some of the fierce, distract-
ing power of D.H. Lawrence's masterpiece, *Women in Love.*"
Kirkus

"A small gem of a novel that's filled with more crucial questions
about the meaning of history than a hundred textbooks."
The Boston Globe

"Nearly perfect prose…almost endlessly quotable."
Tricycle

"… Doctor Zhivago meeting The Odessa Files."
The Milwaukee Journal Sentinel

"Melnyczuk is a master at sustaining intrigue…It's a beautiful novel,
and redemptive in its own way."
Carmela Ciaruru, *The Los Angeles Times*

Some Other Books by PFP / AJAR Contemporaries

a four-sided bed - Elizabeth Searle

A Russian Requiem - Roland Merullo

Ambassador of the Dead - Askold Melnyczuk

Blind Tongues - Sterling Watson

Celebrities in Disgrace (eBook version only) - Elizabeth Searle

Demons of the Blank Page - Roland Merullo

Fighting Gravity - Peggy Rambach

"Gifted: An Indestructibles Christmas Story"-
Matthew Phillion

Girl to Girl: The Real Deal on Being A Girl Today-Anne Driscoll

"Invitations: A Story of Thanksgiving" - Peter Sarno

"Last Call" (eBook "single") - Roland Merullo

Leaving Losapas - Roland Merullo

Lunch with Buddha - Roland Merullo

Make A Wish But Not For Money - Suzanne Strempek Shea

Music In and On the Air - Lloyd Schwartz

My Ground Trilogy - Joseph Torra

Passion for Golf: In Pursuit of the Innermost Game - Roland Merullo

Revere Beach Boulevard - Roland Merullo

Revere Beach Elegy: A Memoir of Home & Beyond - Roland Merullo

Rinpoche's Remarkable Ten-Week Weight Loss Clinic -
Roland Merullo

Taking the Kids to Italy - Roland Merullo

Talk Show - Jaime Clarke

Temporary Sojourner - Tony Eprile

the Book of Dreams - Craig Nova